WARRIOR BOY

VIRGINIA CLAY

Chicken House

2 PALMER STREET, FROME, SOMERSET BA11 1DS

Text © Virginia Clay 2018
Illustration © Kerry Hyndman

First published in Great Britain in 2018
Chicken House
2 Palmer Street
Frome, Somerset BA11 1DS
United Kingdom
www.chickenhousebooks.com

Cover and interior design by Steve Wells
Typeset by Dorchester Typesetting Group Ltd
Printed and bound in Great Britain by CPI Group (UK) Ltd, Croydon CR0 4YY

The paper used in this Chicken House book is made from
wood grown in sustainable forests.

1 3 5 7 9 10 8 6 4 2

British Library Cataloguing in Publication data available.

PB ISBN 978-1-911490-37-1
eISBN 978-1-911490-61-6

For Justin, Amelia and PJ

Reto oreeto olaashe lengeteng'ai
Earth, animals, people – all are one

The African plain lay wide open in front of him – hot as hell, dry as death.

Limbs stiff with fear and readiness, lungs burning with fatigue. His shallow, uneven breaths brought no relief – merely pain and yet more dust. He tried to swallow, but the sides of his throat stuck together for a moment. No water, not even a breeze to cool his parched skin.

Only the hot, hard stare of the lion before him penetrated the haze.

Never look a predator in the eye . . .

Too late. Its amber eyes bore into him, scanning for fear, finding terror.

And then it moved.

As the animal crouched down and set him in its sights, he realized there was only one thing left to do – the worst possible thing in this situation.

Run.

CHAPTER 1

'Yes, I know it's freezing outside,' exclaimed Ms Matthews, 'but please take your coats off in class, otherwise you won't feel the benefit. Right! Today we are learning about the sucking chest wound.'

A wave of sniggers rippled around the room, but Ben didn't join in. Out of all the lessons at The Hill, emergency first aid was the only one worth taking seriously. There were never any tests or homework, and for forty magical minutes Ben could dream that he had made it to medical school.

'Who here has ever seen a gunshot wound?' Ms Matthews continued. The students looked around at each other, nervous grins spreading across their faces.

'OK then, who knows someone who has been stabbed or shot?' Three or four hands were raised tentatively. Ben wondered if they were genuine – his neighbourhood wasn't *that* bad.

Ms Matthews cleared her throat. 'A sucking chest wound occurs when the chest cavity is pierced, the pressure balance is disrupted, and the control of air, in and out of the lung, is lost. Oxygen cannot reach the brain, the victim becomes unconscious very quickly, and they will probably die if they don't receive help from YOU!'

She pointed at Jake and Liam – the McAllister twins – who had already been moved to the front before they could cause any trouble. They jumped slightly, then elbowed each other in the ribs, their faces flushing.

'Statistics tell us that by the time you leave school, every one of you will know someone who has been shot or stabbed. Just a reality of growing up in this part of London, I'm afraid. So concentrate, please, class – what you learn now could save someone's life.'

Ben's dad had saved a life before he'd lost his own. *What it would feel like to be a hero*, wondered Ben, *to be the one everyone looked up to for a change?*

'OK!' said Ms Matthews. 'Take out your school ID, and put it on the desk in front of you.' She strode around the classroom, checking everyone had followed her instructions, then stopped in front of Ben.

'This,' she said, pointing at the ID card in Ben's hand, 'is your best friend for a sucking chest wound.'

'What, Ben Olmoran, Miss?' said Liam McAllister, and Ben knew that a joke about his name was coming next. 'All-Moron? He's no one's best friend!'

Not-very-funny name jokes were about as far as the McAllisters ever went with Ben, but he was well aware that it wasn't like this for everyone.

His rich brown skin and soft, sandy-tipped curls were features that he shared with several other kids in the school, but Ben's eyes were a dark yellow colour, like old gold and his voice sounded more like he was from Harrow than Hackney. Ordinarily, the McAllisters would destroy someone like him, but he was pretty sure the reason they didn't, was because of his dad.

Ms Matthews marched back towards the twins and picked up Jake's ID from the desk in front of him. He folded his arms and stared at her. 'This card,' she continued, unfazed, 'or a credit card, or your bus pass, is all you need to save someone's life when they've been shot or stabbed in the chest. But before I tell you what to do with it, can anyone guess how you recognize a sucking chest wound?'

'There's a vampire running away from the body, Miss?' quipped Liam, and the class erupted. But Ben thought about the question. It must be the sound, he thought – a sucking sound.

'It's the sound of sucking, of course!' said Ms Matthews. 'There will be bright red, frothy blood bubbling from the wound, but the sound is the giveaway.'

Ben's stomach rose into his throat. No one at school knew about his phobia. They wouldn't understand, so he kept it quiet.

Blood.

Just the thought of it was enough to make him dizzy, but as long as he didn't see it, he probably wouldn't faint. He just wished Ms Matthews would stop talking about it. Today was his birthday and if there was one day in the year when he'd like to forget about blood – this was it.

'So,' continued Ms Matthews, 'once you have

identified it as a sucking chest wound, all you need to do is clear the area – which might involve ripping the person's shirt – then you cover the wound with the card and hold it down as firmly as possible. A card like this is good because it forms a tight seal. If you use something soft like a T-shirt, it will be sucked into the hole.'

There were a few snorts of disgust, but most of the class were concentrating now, imagining themselves as lifesavers.

'Finally,' she said, 'you call an ambulance or have someone else do it, keeping the card in place until a paramedic says it's OK to let go.'

As she went over the steps again with the class, Ben began to relax – the immediate danger had most likely passed.

'So, we have established that wounds need pressure to stop the bleeding, but how would you know it was a more serious arterial injury and not just a vein that had been ruptured?' she asked.

Lyra Cohen's hand shot into the air. 'The blood would pour out, Miss?'

Ben's stomach began to churn again.

'Yes,' agreed the teacher, 'it would definitely pour

out, faster than blood from a vein, but sometimes it might even squirt.' The class was silent now, and Ben was convinced they must be able to hear the sound of his heart thumping against his ribs. 'Arterial blood coming out of a wound can reach amazing distances,' Ms Matthews added, reaching for a large plastic water shooter that was lying on her desk.

Then, as she raised it in the air, Ben could see that it was filled, not with water, but a thicker red liquid. His arms and legs went ice-cold.

'This toy gun is filled with stage blood,' she continued. 'I am going to fire it at the whiteboard to show you just how powerful arterial blood can be. How far back do you think I should stand?' she asked the class. Most people opted for the first row and Ms Matthews obliged them by standing there for a few moments. But then she turned dramatically and marched away from the first row, past the second and eventually she took her position next to Ben, on the third.

'The furthest recorded distance for an arterial blood spurt is four metres,' she said. 'Like this!'

Crouching suddenly, she fired the shooter in the direction of the whiteboard. As the bright red paint hit its pristine canvas, the class exploded into whoops and shouts of 'Sick!' and 'No way!'

But no one had noticed that a little bit of fake blood had squirted out of the back of the gun and landed on Ben's face.

He automatically wiped it away with his forearm, then glanced down at his shirt sleeve. The scarlet paint against the bright white cotton was dazzling, almost beautiful. And that was all it took.

Everything around him seemed to slow down, voices deepened and his face, like his limbs, turned to ice. He tried repeating, 'It's just paint, it's just paint,' under his breath, but suddenly felt like he might be sick.

He lurched to his feet. As he did so, his chair screeched backwards, and several people turned to find Ben swaying like a cartoon skyscraper. They began pointing at him and nudging each other, drawing yet more attention to Ben's stricken face.

A wave of dizziness swam through him, and the sea of faces now leering at him became strangely grotesque, stretching and dripping like molten wax. He rubbed his eyes, but it just made everything more blurred.

As his field of vision narrowed, a high-pitched

ringing sound grew in his ears. The two things seemed to be related somehow, like an unseen force was squeezing his eyeballs into dark tunnels and making them squeal in pain.

Then finally, as the last splinter of light in Ben's eyes was extinguished, his legs folded beneath him, pulling the rest of his body with them in a slow-motion slide to the floor.

CHAPTER 2

Ben's mum stopped the car outside their flat and they both sat for a moment, listening to the sound of the rain on the roof and the windscreen wipers flicking back and forth. They hadn't spoken since his mum had come to collect him from school, when she had said, 'I'm sorry, my love!' but Ben had said nothing at all; even if he'd had any words, it would have taken an enormous feat of strength to get them out.

'Come on,' she said eventually, turning off the engine. 'Granny's making your birthday tea and I'm expecting a call from Kenya in about five minutes.'

'Kenya?' Ben's heart leapt into his mouth. 'Why?'

She turned to look at him – her mad-professor blonde hair was in its usual wild state but her soft, hazel eyes had tears balancing on the edges. 'Chifu,' she said, 'the last great-grandfather elephant in Kenya, has just been brutally murdered for his tusks by poachers. I knew him years ago when I was filming with your father.'

Ben's mum had made lots of conservation films; Barack Obama had presented her with an award for one of them and Ben had even got to meet him. He had felt so proud of his mum that day, but he still didn't understand why she was so crazy about elephants.

'Sorry, Mum.' he said. She smiled gently, and a tear escaped from her eye.

'A conservation organization wants me to make a film about it,' she said. 'To show people what's happening and try and bring an end to poaching.'

'Are you going to do it?'

She sighed. 'I said yes to them this morning, but now I'm not so sure. I haven't been back to Kenya since . . .'

Ben couldn't remember the first time his mum had spoken about his dad. He felt like he'd always known how they met – she was making a documentary in the Maasai Mara and he, a local warrior, had been employed as a guard, protecting her from both lions and poachers. But how he'd died – that was a different matter. Ben had asked her for months before she actually gave in and told him, but then he'd wished she hadn't.

She had described how they were out on a night shoot, when a lion had attacked the film crew. Although Ben's dad had managed to distract it, the animal had lashed at him with razor-sharp claws. They were so far out in the bush that he had bled to death before help could reach them.

'Well you've got to go back sometime, haven't you?' Ben said, trying to push the image from his mind. 'And I could go with you. You'll need a big, strong Maasai to protect you.'

She reached across and tousled his soft, caramel curls; he pretended to be annoyed by it, as usual.

'But seriously, though, Mum, can I come?'

'Oh, Ben!' she replied. 'It's a work trip, and you know that means I wouldn't have time to spend with you.'

'But it's my birthday today.'

'What? Is it?' she said, her eyes sparkling. 'I'd forgotten. But then you probably don't care about presents now that you're a teenager, right?'

'That's not what I meant,' said Ben, his cheeks warming slightly. 'You said you'd take me to Kenya when I turned thirteen.'

'And I will – we have a whole year to go yet!'

'But why not now? It's half-term tomorrow. I could visit my family while you make your film.'

'That's what Granny said.'

'Maybe she's right!'

'Ben, it's so dangerous. It's not just the wild animals. There are men out there with guns, killing elephants because their tusks are worth a lot of money. If anyone gets in their way—'

'Yeah, but that means *you'd* be in danger. Am I supposed to sit at home on my own while you're being shot at by poachers?'

'You won't be on your own – Granny would come and stay with you.'

'And that's a good idea because . . .?'

'Well maybe you could go to Granny and Grandpa's instead? We could ask the cousins over.'

Ben rolled his eyes. The idea of being stuck with

that lot, going on about their latest rugby and hockey victories . . . 'You're not exactly selling it, Mum.'

'Oh, well!' she sighed. 'I don't know if I've got the guts to go back so soon, anyway.'

'Soon? It's been thirteen years!'

She smiled at him. 'Look, Ben, it's not just the danger thing, it's also the money. Flights are expensive!'

'What about Granny?' he asked.

'What *about* her?'

'She's got lots of money! If she thinks I should go too, why don't we ask her to help?'

'We could, but . . .' Ben's mum took his hand in hers and he shivered slightly at the coolness of it. The heat that had built up in the car from their drive, seemed to have drained away. 'Ben,' she said quietly, 'suppose Granny had bought you a plane ticket. Have you thought about what would actually happen in Kenya?'

'What do you mean?'

She let go of his hand and Ben pulled his hoodie up over his head.

'Well,' she said, 'you're the only son of the great warrior, and they haven't met you yet. Do you think they'll just smile and say hello?'

He didn't know what to say.

'No, Ben. There will be a huge welcoming ceremony with dancing and singing and their finest young bull will be slaughtered. But not just that . . .' She took a deep breath. 'Blood will be taken from a heifer and you'll be expected to drink it. Not a lot – just a mouthful – but how will you even look at it, let alone drink it? You can't cut your finger without passing out.'

Suddenly, Ben felt like the ground beneath his seat was no longer solid, as though they were floating in a boat on the ocean. He was at once minuscule and then too big for the confines of the car.

'But it's my family . . .' he said in a small voice.

Ben's mum gazed at him. She had that look in her eye – like she was just about to hug him. Ben braced himself – but then her phone rang.

'That'll be Kenya,' she said, rummaging in her handbag and trying to open the car door at the same time. 'I need to take this. Let's get you inside – it's freezing!'

CHAPTER 3

Ben flipped on the light switch and stood with his back against the door. Though his bedroom was small, it was a cocoon of colourful memorabilia from a country he had never visited. His eyes fell, as they always did, on the centre of it all – a photograph of his Kenyan father.

Ben took a step towards the narrow chest of drawers where the picture rested and instinctively lifted the wooden picture frame up to his nose. It was made out of an olive tree from his father's Kenyan village, that had been cut down when he died. Ben wondered if it had always felt so silky, or if it had become that way through constant handling. As a toddler, when other children had comfort blankets, Ben had held on to this little picture, rubbing the frame against his nose, thumbs and forefingers, enjoying its earthy smell.

The image showed his father wearing the traditional red toga of the Maasai tribe, but none of the few people who had ever seen it had laughed at the fact his dad was wearing a 'dress'. Ben smiled at the thought. He knew every detail of the photo, but he stared all the same, and the dark face, daubed with white paint, gazed back. Sometimes, if he looked for long enough, it seemed to move; the lion's-mane headdress might ripple slightly in the breeze, or the long spear in his father's hand would sparkle in the bright sun.

Ben returned the picture to its usual position, then, in one stride, leapt across to his bed and climbed under the duvet, fully clothed. He closed his eyes and the McAllister twins leered at him from behind his eyelids. How was he ever going to show his face in school again?

He opened his eyes and glanced over at his father's picture, then felt a pang of shame as he wondered what his warrior dad would have made of his performance earlier.

There was a tap at the door; it creaked open and a

wild mop of blonde hair appeared, with his mum's face attached to it. 'Dinner's nearly ready,' she said gently. 'But I thought you might like to open this first.' She placed a small present, with a card attached to it, proudly on the bed in front of him.

'Thanks,' he said sheepishly, feeling guilty for hiding in his room on his birthday. He opened the card first, to make up for it.

My darling Ben, it read. *Happy birthday! I think this is what you wanted. Lots of love, Mum.*

He picked up the present and a wave of excitement bubbled up inside him. He had been dropping hints about an iPhone since last summer when, on a geography school trip to the Lake District, everyone else had had a phone except him. But he'd never thought for a second that his mum would actually get him one.

'Open it, then,' she said, and with one deft movement Ben tore off the paper. The box tumbled out on to the bed and lay between them, full of promise: a clean, crisp shade of white. But that was all it had in common with an iPhone.

As he turned the box over, an unpronounceable brand name shouted loudly in garish green and yellow, and it dawned on Ben that he had seen it before. He and his friend Finn had laughed at it in the phone shop, calling it the apatosaurus of the phone world. Now he wished that he could wrap it back up and tell his mum he would open it later.

'Happy?' she said.

He nodded and looked at the floor.

'Ben,' she said, reaching for his hand and squeezing it tightly, 'I am so sorry about what happened at school today.'

'It's OK.'

'Well, it must have been awful, but I want you to know that I'm going to take the job in Kenya and if you want to come with me,' she paused, 'that's fine!'

Ben glanced at the image of his father – *he* didn't look like someone who was afraid of blood.

'It's all right, Mum,' Ben said. 'Maybe you're right. I can always go later.'

'Oh, sweetheart! Have you changed your mind?'

He held his gaze on the floor.

'Well that's fine too,' she said, her voice brighter suddenly. 'Kenya's not going anywhere. Maybe you'll feel ready next year. Come on, Granny's cooking up a storm, let's go and eat!'

*

'Happy birthday, Benedict!' cried Ben's granny as Ben sloped into the kitchen. Then came the inevitable powdery hug – he was easily taller than her, but she still insisted on it. He didn't really mind, though; it was something constant, unchanging.

'Right!' she said. 'As it's your birthday, I've made your favourite. Sit down, then!'

He did as he was told, and she plonked a steaming plate of well-done fillet steak and chips in front of him, with a huge glass of Coke and not a trace of vegetables anywhere. Then she pushed a bottle of ketchup towards him with a satisfied smile, knowing she had completed everything perfectly. Ben's granny didn't approve of fizzy drinks or ketchup, and she certainly never allowed them in her house in the country, but this just made them even more of a treat.

'Thanks, Gran,' he said, squirting a pool of red sauce on to his plate. For a split second his mind flashed back to the image of the red paint on the whiteboard, but he was too hungry now to care. Fainting always made him feel weak for a while, but this was quickly replaced by ravenous hunger.

'So, what happened at school today?' she asked. 'Did that silly teacher *have* to repaint the classroom while you were still in it?'

'It wasn't her fault,' he mumbled through a mouthful of food.

'Well, at least it's half-term now and you don't have to go back for a while. You'll see, they'll have forgotten all about it.'

'I wish!'

'And what about Kenya?' she continued. 'Mum tells me you would like to go.'

'Well, actually—'

'And I agree! You can't stay here with a silly old fool like me, whilst your mum is saving elephants and wrestling poachers in Africa!'

'What's that about elephant wrestling?' said his mum, joining them at last.

'Ben was just telling me how much he wants to go to Kenya.'

'What?' said his mum. 'But I thought you'd changed your—'

'Granny!' said Ben, looking up at her in disbelief. She had a twinkle in her eye. 'I was going to say, I'm not sure.'

'Now, what on earth have you got to be unsure about?'

'A lot actually! Like how is anyone in my dad's tribe ever going to accept me when I can't even look at blood, never mind drink it?' For a moment he was afraid his dinner might come up again.

'It's OK, darling,' said his mum.

'Nonsense, Kate,' scolded his granny. 'It's not OK. Listen, Ben, they're your *family*! Suppose I was meeting you for the first time on your thirteenth birthday and I'd baked you a cake covered in sprinkles. You might be allergic to sprinkles and throw up all over my shoes, but do you think I'd care? I would just be happy to meet you at last.'

Ben smiled. It was impossible to tell what she was going to say next.

'Also, maybe they can help you.'

'How?' he said, stuffing a forkful of steak in his mouth.

'Perhaps they'll know how to deal with your fear.' His granny sat down across the table, grabbed both his hands and stared straight into his eyes. Why were the women in his life always doing this? He hadn't even finished eating yet.

'Ben!' she said. 'You want to be a doctor, don't you?'

Ben's eyes opened wide and he stopped chewing.

'Oh, don't look at me like that, I'm your grand-mother and it's my job to know these things.' He could feel a warmth creeping into his cheeks. She carried on: 'If your Kenyan family has the secret to helping you, and you don't go and find out what it is, you will always be sorry.'

He swallowed. 'But what if they don't?'

She stared at Ben for a moment, as if considering her next move, then turned to his mum, suddenly. 'Kate!' she said. 'Did you print off that thingummybob?'

Ben's mum sighed. 'In the drawer,' she said, gesturing with her chin. Ben's granny leapt to her feet, opened the drawer and pulled out a piece of printed A4 paper.

'I wondered,' Granny said, folding the paper into a rudimentary aeroplane, 'whether you might like to go and find out for yourself!' She launched the missile in Ben's direction and it landed perfectly by the side of his plate.

Ben looked at his mum – her lips were pressed together in a tight line.

'Don't you want to know what's in it?' asked Granny.

Ben unfolded the paper, and despite all the wrinkles

from where it had been folded, he could still make out the words OLMORAN, BENEDICT. Then underneath was printed tomorrow's date and the words: LONDON HEATHROW TO NAIROBI, JOMO KENYATTA INTERNATIONAL AIRPORT.

'Happy birthday, Ben!' his granny said. Then she reached into the cupboard behind her and pulled out a cake iced in black, red and green – the colours of the Kenyan flag.

'Do I have a choice?' he asked.

'You always have a choice!' she said, lighting the candles, then she stood back to admire her handiwork. 'Go on then! Make a wish!' she urged. 'You're not allergic to sprinkles, are you?'

CHAPTER 4

'There will be some turbulence,' the pilot had said.

Ben decided this was something of an understatement as his stomach was left behind for the third time since they had begun their descent. Pockets of hot air, the passengers were told, would begin reflecting up from the earth's surface after midday, and this might bring about some bumpiness. You could say that again. Turbulence wasn't so noticeable in a Boeing 747, like the one that flew them from London to Nairobi, but this tiny little caravan plane to the Maasai Mara was a different matter altogether. A couple of times, his backside had even lost contact with the seat.

Ben gazed down at the dry, mustard-yellow savannah

below. He had never before seen such an expanse of land, and as the plane banked to the right he was relieved to notice there were hills in the distance, giving the vast plain a kind of boundary.

'Look! There's the airstrip,' shouted Jez, the crew's fiery-haired cameraman from the seat in front.

Ben looked out of his tiny window and could just make out a long, straight, terracotta-coloured scar stretching across the ground. He had no fear of flying – or landing, for that matter – but as the little plane positioned itself for the final descent, Ben found himself tightly gripping the arm of his seat. Perhaps his granny was right and the family really could help him beat his fear of blood. But what if they couldn't? What then?

The light aircraft bounced down on to the airstrip and quickly taxied to a standstill, then the engine was cut and everyone started piling out. Jez climbed out first, followed by Phil the sound man, who might have looked like a pirate with his enormous black beard, but could usually be found standing quietly behind Jez, listening intently.

Ben glanced across the aisle at his mum; her fore-head was patterned with hard ridges that softened when he caught her eye.

'Come on, then,' she said, and gestured for him to pass in front of her.

He jumped from the last rung of the tiny ladder into the dry red dirt, creating a mini dust cloud that sent the crew nervously clucking around the camera cases like mother hens counting their chicks. When the dust had settled, Ben took a deep breath, replacing the stale air in his lungs with this new air of Africa – earthy and fragrant, warm and spicy. He closed his eyes and let the sun soak into his skin.

'Come on, Twiglet!' urged Jez. 'Lend a hand!'

Ben heaved a rucksack on to his back, then grabbed a holdall and followed the crew towards the Land Cruiser that was waiting on the edge of the airstrip. Two dark-skinned men stood next to the vehicle. The first was wearing a short-sleeved khaki suit and grinning at them broadly, but Ben was immediately captivated by the man standing next to him. Perhaps it was the vermilion toga that grabbed his attention, or the fact that the man's neck, ears, waist and ankles were adorned with brightly beaded jewellery. There was something about the way he watched them intensely as they approached, that stirred up the butterflies in

Ben's stomach.

His mum squeezed his free hand briefly, and though it was probably meant to comfort him, the telltale dampness of it just left him feeling more nervous.

'Welcome back, you lot!' called the man in the khaki suit as they drew near. They all put their bags down and greeted each other warmly with hugs and back slaps, as the Maasai man stood at a slight distance.

'Trevor,' said Ben's mum proudly to the first man, 'this is my son, Benedict.'

'Welcome to the Maasai Mara, Benedict!' said Trevor. 'I'll be looking after you whilst you're here – if there's anything you need or want to know, just ask me!'

'Thank you,' Ben replied, acutely aware that, during this whole exchange, the Maasai man was staring at him. Ben had never enjoyed being the centre of attention before, and it was no different now. There was a megawatt intensity pouring from the man's face that made Ben feel like he was standing in a searchlight. It was excruciatingly difficult to meet his eyes – and when Ben eventually did, he found he could only manage a few seconds before having to look away.

'Hello, Senteu,' said Kate hesitantly. Her voice sounded strangely small, but it drew the Maasai man's attention away from Ben, and once the focus was off, he could look back at this man, Senteu. Ben noticed an air of hardness about him, as if he was someone unused to kindness. His body was as upright as a statue, and when he turned to Ben's mum, he raised his chin slightly and his face seemed as though it might have been chiselled out of stone.

'Kate,' he replied, coolly.

Trevor and Senteu could not have been more different. While one beamed, the other smouldered; the first was an open door, the second a wall.

'This is Ben,' his mum said.

'Yes.' Senteu turned his gaze back towards Ben.

'Ben –' his mum paused – 'This is Senteu . . . your uncle.'

All at once Ben felt like the ground might give way under his feet. Senteu continued to stare at him as if he was searching for something, or perhaps waiting for Ben to speak. His face was like a pool with a calm surface, barely hiding the swirling depths beneath. And as they gazed at each other, it seemed like the earth itself was holding its breath, until at last, Trevor broke the silence with a clap of his hands, making Ben jump.

'Right, then! Let's get going!' he exclaimed.

Senteu effortlessly shinned up on to the roof of the 4x4 and gestured to the crew to pass him pieces of luggage, which he then secured on to the roof rack. Ben watched as his uncle's lean and muscular body twisted and flexed in the sunlight, and he wondered if his father had moved like that.

The vehicle was loaded up and strapped down in no time, and the crew began to climb in. 'In you get, Twiglet!' said Jez, giving Ben a helpful nudge into the back of the open-sided safari car. Ben was amazed to find that his legs didn't give way.

'You all right there, darling?' asked his mum from the front, as she fumbled for a packet of tissues in her handbag. Ben nodded, but she didn't see it; Phil gave him a reassuring squeeze on the arm.

Trevor got in next to Kate, and Senteu swung into the driver's seat. As the warm air was disturbed around him, Ben caught his uncle's overwhelmingly powerful scent. It was a strange mixture of things – sweat, of course, but also a kind of animal smell that Ben couldn't name. There was something strangely comforting about it though, like that was exactly how a Maasai *should* smell.

'Right, ladies and gents!' said Trevor, placing his hand on Senteu's shoulder, and releasing a waft of his own, more synthetic, deodorant smell. 'This is Senteu, our distinguished guard, guide and driver.'

Senteu twisted round in his seat so everyone could see him, momentarily revealing an arrow-shaped scar on the back of his shoulder as he did so. Ben wondered what injury might have left such a mark as Senteu pulled at his toga slightly, deftly re-covering the scar.

'He's going to help us find what we're looking for – elephants or poachers –' Trevor continued, 'and do his best to keep us out of trouble with both.'

The others laughed and introduced themselves to Senteu, but Ben still had no voice. Was his uncle disappointed with him? Ben wondered if there was something he should have done or said differently, and his stomach lurched as he thought about meeting the rest of the family.

Thankfully, the drive to the camp was a great distraction – like watching a wildlife documentary in 3D. After about a mile or so, Trevor invited Ben to sit on top of the vehicle with his legs dangling down through the sun hatch so he could look out for animals.

Now and again Senteu would stop the vehicle so they could scan for wildlife through their binoculars. 'We haven't seen a lion for about a week now,' said Trevor. 'They seem to have gone into hiding.'

'That's OK,' Kate replied. 'We're here to film the elephants, and I'm sure we'll find some of those.'

When they first spotted the herd, a hush fell upon everyone in the car. At first Ben couldn't understand why the chatter underneath him had suddenly stopped, or why everyone was staring and silently pointing in the same direction. But then he spied them – a group of grey ghosts moving steadily across the horizon, changing shape now and again as they opened and closed their enormous ears.

Without warning, Senteu drove off towards them, almost causing Ben to fall off the roof, but thanks to the constant undercurrent of nerves, he'd been holding on tightly. They drove closer and closer at breakneck speed, eventually coming to a stop much nearer to the animals than Ben had imagined possible.

He'd always known that elephants were big – who didn't? But he'd never had anything to compare them to before. In the flesh, they were gargantuan, towering over him as he sat perched on top of the car.

Some of the babies, on the other hand, were quite small and looked a little like Eeyore, with their saggy ears and droopy back legs. But the largest member of the group had to be the same size as a dustbin lorry, though not as smelly or noisy, and much more peaceful to watch.

Senteu cut the engine, and as Ben's hearing adjusted to the quiet, he noticed that the growl of the Land Cruiser's engine had been replaced by a deeper murmuring from the elephants. When the largest animal had walked past them – only metres away – Ben realized it was the sound of its stomach rumbling, like an old tractor engine turning over inside an empty barn.

But the thing that struck Ben most of all was that despite the elephants' enormous size, there was an air of goodness about them, as though they meant no harm to anyone. Even when they were pulling up bushes and pushing over trees, they seemed to do it gently. There was a constant communication between them too. Now and again, they would feel for each other with their trunks – sniffing, playing, reassuring

– like a family of oversized, off-duty clowns enjoying each other's company.

It was impossible to tell how long they stayed there, with the gentle giants moving slowly amongst them, but when Ben's mum had reached up and squeezed his foot eventually, he had felt thankful for the enforced silence. This was what she loved and now he understood why.

CHAPTER 5

When they arrived at the camp, several more Maasai helpers appeared, and their luggage was removed from the vehicle within the time it took everyone to get out. Tiny little glasses of ice-cold pink juice appeared as if by magic, and everyone except Ben drained them immediately, making loud smacking noises with their lips. He braved a small sip. Flavours of strawberry, raspberry and peach exploded into his mouth, like a fruit sherbet ice-lolly in a glass. He glanced around to see if there might be any more, and noticed that Trevor was watching him, smiling.

'Iced hibiscus tea,' he said. 'We make it ourselves. Good, huh?' Then, before Ben could answer with anything other than a nod, Trevor gathered everyone around him. 'For the sake of those who have never been here before,' he said, winking at Ben, 'all the staff in the camp are members of the local Maasai community. It's normally tourists who stay here, and they pay a lot of money to go and visit the Maasai village. If the elephants die out, the tourists stop coming and everybody suffers. The Maasai understand what you're doing with your film, and you are most welcome!'

On the plane, Ben's mum had explained that they would be staying in a lodge just outside his father's village. Ben glanced around at the faces of some of the camp staff going about their business – could there be a family resemblance?

Suddenly, a group of Maasai boys and girls trooped in and began organizing themselves into rows as if they were about to perform something. Eventually they stopped moving and an eerie quiet fell upon them. Every one of the children looked to Senteu, who remained expressionless for several moments. Then, as if some small thing had satisfied him, he nodded and a rhythmical chanting began from within the group.

At first it was a steady bass line of throaty grunts, all the bodies undulating in time to the music, as if they were pushing out the sound with each ripple of their collective sea. Then, when this was well established, one of the older girls sang a piercingly high tune over the top of it all, like a strange sea bird soaring over the ocean.

After a while, Ben noticed there were goosebumps prickling on his arms. It was as if the shadow of a distant memory was beginning to form somewhere inside him, but before he could grasp hold of it, the choir stopped and everyone started clapping and cheering.

This time yesterday, he had been in a taxi driving through the cold, dark streets of London, and now he was here, with the sun warming his face, feeling like he was in a film.

As the choir disbanded, Ben noticed one of the boys run straight up to Senteu and bend at the waist, offering him the top of his head. Senteu touched it gently, his face softening slightly. Then just as Ben was wondering who this boy could be to have changed Senteu's expression so radically, the boy turned, looked at Ben and broke into the most enormous grin.

'Whassup, Ben?' he said, bouncing over with his right arm held out to the side.

Ben lifted his hand to shake the boy's, but it was met with a hearty slap instead. Then Ben was pulled into a chest bump, followed by what he could have sworn was a kiss on the cheek. This was then repeated on the other side, far too slowly for comfort.

'How do you know my name?' asked Ben.

'Ah, come on, cuz, I'd recognize you anywhere,' laughed the boy, slapping Ben on the shoulder. 'My name's Kipat Masikonde Olmoran, but you can call me Kip. The big guy who drove you is my dad, Senteu Lemeikoki Olmoran. He was *your* dad's brother. That makes us cousins, man!'

Although Kipat wore the red toga of the Maasai, he sounded anything but traditional. His voice had a subtle accent that Ben had never heard before, but it sounded more like a TV presenter's than what Ben would have ever expected from a Maasai.

'Welcome!' his cousin continued. 'I'm so pumped to see you, I've been up since four this morning.' He shifted from foot to foot with excitement, his toga swinging around him as he moved, making him look like a Roman centurion preparing to breakdance.

'How did you know we were coming?' asked Ben. 'Did my mum tell you?'

'No! Ngai told us.'

'Who?'

'Ngai. God told us you were coming.'

'God told you . . .' Ben's brain jammed.

'Well, yeah,' Kip said. 'Because you didn't reply to any of our letters, the elders decided we had to ask Ngai. We needed to know what to do with the cattle that belonged to your dad. Ngai told us you would come for them when you were of age. And here you are.'

'You wrote me letters?' Ben asked quietly, not knowing which was more bewildering – the letters, the cows or a talking god.

'Yeah, bro!' said Kip proudly. 'Me and Granny Koko wrote every month for the last year. You mean you never got them?'

Ben shook his head.

'What! Your mum wrote back a few times but she never answered our question about the cows, so we—'

'—had to ask God,' whispered Ben, as though the wind had been knocked out of him. *Why hadn't she told him about this?*

'Whatever, man, you have thirty beautiful cows waiting for you. Come and meet them and the rest of the family tomorrow, at noon. We've waited a long time for you. There's going to be a *big* celebration.'

'OK, thanks,' said Ben, wondering if his nerves were showing.

Kip glanced over at his father, who beckoned him with an almost imperceptible nod of the head.

'Laters!' he said, pulling Ben into another double chest bump. 'It's good to finally meet you, man!' Then he was gone, running to catch up with the others, who were already a scarlet sea in the distance.

'Who was that?' said Ben's mum, smiling at him and putting her arm around his shoulder.

'My cousin, I think,' replied Ben.

'So *that's* Kipat?'

'Yeah, he said I can call him Kip.'

'Oh, great!' she said, her voice suddenly sounding overly cheerful. 'What did he say?'

'He invited us to the village tomorrow.' Ben swallowed. 'I've no idea how to get there, though.'

'Don't worry! I think I can remember the way, and if not, I'm sure Senteu will come and guide us.'

They stood together in silence and watched Ben's new-found cousin and uncle walking away. Ben wondered whether he should ask his mum about the letters. It seemed strange that she hadn't told him about them, especially seeing as they never kept secrets from each other. But he decided to wait until everything was straight in his mind first – there was so much to think about.

'Come on,' Mum said, turning to walk inside. 'Let's get settled in.'

CHAPTER 6

On the plane, when Ben's mum and the crew had been discussing 'the camp', Ben had thought of his school trip to the Lake District with tents, sleeping bags on the ground, baked beans out of a tin and freezing cold showers. The reality could not have been more different.

From outside, the lodge just looked like a thatched cottage with a pointy roof, but the moment Ben walked through the reception and into the main area, his gaze was magnetically drawn upwards. The ceiling extended so high that he gave a little soundless 'Wow!' and he imagined his breath floating upwards like a cloud. He looked down and noticed the whole area was made up of different levels, connected by various steps. Some were wide and deep, some short and narrow, but they all seemed to be carved out of the rock. And the best part of it all was that the back of the building was open, revealing a panoramic view of the wilderness.

On the left-hand side was what looked like a dining area, with tables constructed of knotted and gnarled pieces of shiny wood, each looking like a sculpture in an art gallery. The chairs were covered on their seat pads and backs by a rich brown leather and finished with shining brass studs.

Across from the dining area, on the right-hand side, was a long bar made out of the same elegantly twisted wood as the dining tables. As Ben looked around, he could see this wood was everywhere – in the furniture, the beams overhead and the posts that held everything up. It was like some crazy old professor had built a home for himself amidst the roots of an ancient tree.

A smiling barman was already lining up a row of ice-cold beers for the crew as they counted all their cases for the fifteenth time that day. Ben's mum and Jez had sunk into one of the soft-looking sofas around the bar, presumably to discuss their plans for filming.

Plump earth-coloured floor cushions were scattered around them, and golden lanterns hung down from the ceiling. Ben wanted to touch everything, to turn the pages of the glossy coffee-table books, painstakingly placed to look casual. But he just couldn't move. He gazed out through the open sides of the lodge. As far as the eye could see was rolling, parched countryside, punctuated with flat-topped trees that seemed to be growing sideways and looked so typical of Africa as Ben had seen it on the television.

He glanced over at his mum and Jez, relaxing and laughing on the comfortable cushions, taking dewy beer bottles from a waiter with a shiny tray. Without warning, a wave of nerves crashed through him again. Somewhere out there was the rest of his family; he was nearer to them now than he had ever been, thousands of miles nearer, but confusingly he felt further away. He found himself longing for the dreary buildings and streets of London to close around him like a dull but trusted friend.

'It takes some getting used to,' said a voice suddenly at his side, and Ben turned to see Trevor gazing out at the same view. 'I'm from Nairobi and when I first arrived here, I wanted to go home. Imagine! Anyway, now I love it, but home will always be home. Come on, let me show you around.'

Ben was expecting Trevor to show him straight to his room, but instead he was taken to a workshop where a handful of men and women were working on various items: a piece of tent canvas, dining-room chairs, a hanging lantern. One man was sitting at an old-fashioned sewing machine and seemed to be mending some kind of uniform. Everyone looked up and smiled, calling out their greetings in sing-song voices.

'Land Rover or Toyota?' asked Trevor, leading Ben out of one workshop and into a much dirtier one next door, filled with engine parts and tyres. He didn't seem to care whether Ben answered the question or not. 'People are divided over which is best, but the Toyota Land Cruiser has really proved its reliability out here. All our drivers are experts in two things: the local wildlife and the Land Cruiser engine.'

A man in oily overalls looked out from under the bonnet of a 4x4 and smiled at Ben.

'The tourists come here for the wildlife,' said Trevor. 'So we have to have our safari vehicles ready to go at all times. This is one of the most luxurious camps in the Mara and we usually have a lot of celebrities staying here in season. How much do you think it costs per night?'

Ben hesitated, not sure if it was a rhetorical question.

'Go on, guess!' urged Trevor. 'How much – per person, per night – do you think it costs to stay here?'

'A hundred pounds?' offered Ben.

'Try a thousand,' replied Trevor.

There were so many questions flying around in Ben's mind but, afraid of sounding stupid, he decided to stay quiet. This was made easier by the fact that Trevor seemed happy to talk as he continued to show Ben round the perimeter of the camp, and back in through the 'Emergency Route' as he called it. This was quite a grand name for what, in actual fact, was a simple gate in the electric fence at the back of the camp, but it was incredibly well hidden.

'If you didn't know it was there, you wouldn't know it was there,' said Trevor proudly.

Ben couldn't help but wonder why it needed to be such a secret – it wasn't as if they needed to fool the animals or anything. But before he could ask, they arrived at a large tent on a plinth, with steps leading up to a decked veranda.

'Here we are,' Trevor announced. 'Home sweet home!'

CHAPTER 7

‘We thought you would like your own room.’
Trevor slapped Ben on the back. ‘Every
teenage boy needs time away from his mum. Let me
show you what's what.’

Ben was told which water was safe to drink and how
to turn off the lights at night from his bed so he didn't
have to fumble around in the dark. Then Trevor
showed him how to close his tent with a double zip
and a carabiner, to avoid monkeys climbing in and
eating his toothpaste.

‘Oh, and this is the most important thing!’ Trevor
picked up a long decorated spear that was leaning
against one of the pillars on the veranda. ‘If any lions

peer at you from the long grass – or if your mum wants to interrupt your cave time too soon – just throw this at them.' Trevor laughed in the way you would imagine Father Christmas might – from the bottom of his round barrel of a belly. But then he suddenly stopped. 'You know I'm only joking about your mum, right?'

Trevor obviously didn't understand that Ben was much more disturbed by the idea of lions hiding in the grass than his mum checking in on him. How on earth was he supposed to throw a spear? He wouldn't even know which end was which!

'It's wonderful what she's doing with this film, you know,' said Trevor.

'What do you mean?' asked Ben, having found the courage to speak at last.

'The poachers are killing the elephants to sell the ivory. If there are no more elephants, which could happen in your lifetime, there'll be no more tourists. If there are no more tourists, the Maasai will suffer and I'll be out of a job. Your mum is trying to put a stop to that.'

'Are you a Maasai?' asked Ben, gathering confidence.

'No, son! I'm from the Kikuyu tribe. But we are good at recognizing quality, and your mum – well, she's quality.'

Ben realized his mouth was hanging open and so he closed it quickly.

'Come on,' said Trevor, smiling. 'Let's get you back, so she doesn't think I've kidnapped you.'

By the time it came to supper, Ben was so hungry that he devoured two rounds of barbecued chicken, coleslaw and mashed potatoes without stopping for breath. He had even eaten the green beans, and they hadn't poisoned him after all. Then he managed to squeeze in a big pile of pineapple crumble and ice cream.

When he finally sat back in his chair, he noticed that one of the waiters kept looking over at him and laughing with Trevor.

'It's OK, Ben,' said Trevor. 'We were just saying how good it is to have someone who eats with such force. It's a refreshing change to the celebrities we're used to, with their strange dietary requests.'

Ben tried to stifle a nervous grin, and then, rather oddly, a huge yawn took its place. The moment the sun had gone down, the air had become cold surprisingly quickly, and he suddenly realized how tired he was.

He hoped to just slip away, but his mum said loudly, 'You ready for bed, Ben?' And everyone joined in with a chorus of 'Good night! Sleep tight!' Though he could feel his face warming at the attention, he couldn't help but smile – they were such a funny group of people. And he was very grateful when Trevor distracted his mum from walking him to his tent with the promise of some elephant photos, winking conspiratorially over his shoulder as he led her away.

Ben quickly set out along the path to his tent, torch in hand, before his mum could change her mind. Huge moths and other nameless creatures flitted in and out of the beam of light, some bumping against his hand, making him jump a little. Then, just as he was beginning to think how good it felt to be on his own, a hand touched him on the shoulder.

'Hippo!' whispered a deep voice. The hand on his shoulder moved to turn off his torch, and as Ben's eyes adjusted to the darkness he could just make out the shape of a huge hippopotamus crossing the path about ten metres in front of them. Trevor had warned them of the dangers of these seemingly placid beasts. 'One of Africa's biggest killers,' he had said.

When the animal had moved into the darkness

of the bush on the other side of the path, the hand loosened its grip on Ben's shoulder.

'Come!' the guard said, and he led the way silently along a different, hippo-free route to Ben's tent, then dissolved into the darkness as quickly and quietly as he had appeared.

Ben had expected to be sleeping on a mat on the floor, so when Trevor had shown him around earlier, he had been pleasantly surprised to find an actual bed in his tent. And now he was even more amazed to discover it was the most comfortable bed he had ever lain down upon in his entire life. It was so wide that he could have slept sideways without his feet leaving the mattress, and it had a thick duvet and four soft pillows for his tired head to sink into.

The canvas sides of his tent had been rolled up, leaving just a net to protect him from mosquitoes. Ben wondered if it would also protect him from lions, and he sank down so that only his eyes were peeping out of the duvet.

As he lay there, trying to remember every aspect of the day – the plane, the elephants and the amazing camp – his thoughts settled on his uncle Senteu. How could a father and son be so different? Kip had the kind of face that made you want to laugh, but his dad looked like he'd sooner make someone cry than crack a smile.

A bolt of electricity shot through Ben's body as he thought about meeting the rest of the family. Would they be more like Senteu or Kip, he wondered – and, more importantly, would they like him? He tried to picture his grandparents, and how it would be to meet them for the first time, but eventually, despite his attempts to stay awake and plan exactly what he was going to say, he fell into a deep sleep.

CHAPTER 8

Ben had never encountered such heat before. How could somewhere be so cold at night yet so hot in the day? It made him worry about why they had asked him to come at noon. Perhaps it was a test.

When Kip had arrived at the camp instead of Senteu, Ben had felt an enormous sense of relief. 'You ready, bro?' Kip had asked.

'Er...'

'You'll be fine,' he said. 'Just remember to bow your head to your elders – and when children do the same to you, just put your hand on their head. It's how we say hello.'

Ben went hot and cold with the memory of meeting

his uncle yesterday, remembering how he hadn't bowed his head. Perhaps that's why Senteu had seemed so cross, Ben thought.

'Well, that doesn't sound too difficult,' said Ben, trying not to sound as nervous as he felt.

'Exactly! You're going to love it. All the local young people will dance and sing for you and your grandparents will greet you. Then your grandfather will spit on you.'

'What?'

'Yeah, if Koipapi is sure it's really you, he'll spit on you.'

'That's what I thought you said.'

'It's what the elders do to returning warriors. First he'll take a mouthful of honey beer from a gourd—'

'A what?'

'A gourd – it's like a bottle – kind of looks like a baseball bat – anyway, then he'll bless you by spitting the beer in your face.'

'Nice.'

'Yup. Just try not to turn away. You don't have to smile or anything.'

Ben swallowed.

'Next, you'll have a cup of tea in Granny Koko's

house, then there will be a huge barbecue with as much meat as you can eat.' Kip hesitated for a moment, then looked away. 'And that's it.'

Ben didn't know what to say. Apart from the spitting bit, it all sounded quite harmless. Kip had not mentioned anything about blood drinking though. Perhaps they didn't do it any more, thought Ben, hopefully.

But not knowing for sure, that was the worst part. And as they made their way to the village, Ben ran through every possible scenario over and over again in his head, until he thought he might go mad.

Everything about their walk made Ben feel like he had stumbled into one of his grandfather's cowboy films. It was high noon, there was dry dust and tumbleweed everywhere. All it lacked was the sound of clinking spurs and a suitable soundtrack.

It felt like hours, but in reality had probably been about twenty minutes, before they rounded a hill and saw the village below them in the distance.

The *manyatta*, as Kip referred to the little village, consisted of a collection of flat-topped mud huts inside a high circular fence of sticks, without a bit of greenery anywhere to soften the picture. Kip signalled for them to stop, and they all paused on top of the hill. 'Right, this is it. I'll go ahead and tell everyone you're coming. You wait here, until you get the signal.'

'Hang on!' called Ben after him. 'What's the signal?'

'You can't miss it,' he replied. 'You'll hear them.' And off he ran.

They watched him go until he was just a red dot moving in and out of the huts, gathering other red dots as he went.

'You all right?' asked Ben's mum, laying a hand on his shoulder.

'Yup,' Ben replied, untruthfully.

Then suddenly they heard it, a sound to make your blood run cold. Kip was right, it was unmistakable: a wailing noise that grew stronger as more voices were added to it. The moment he heard the sound, Ben remembered learning about it in geography. The teacher had called it 'ululating', and had played audio recordings of it, inviting the students to try and copy it. At the time it had been funny, but the effect was quite different now. Even though he knew it was a call of welcome, he couldn't help feeling as though he was about to be scalped.

'Come on,' said his mum, pushing him gently. 'It's now or never.'

Ben's legs almost gave way, but somehow they carried him down the hill towards the little village.

Dozens of young boys and girls, dripping with decorative beads and metal trinkets, poured out through a hole in the fence and lined up on either side of it. As the women continued to wail and Ben and his mum drew nearer, the young people began to stamp out a rhythm and sing. It was like the welcoming song they'd heard yesterday, but faster and more energetic.

A young girl ran out to meet them, carrying a thin branch with green leaves on it. She bowed her head in front of Ben, and it took him a few moments to remember that he was supposed to touch it. As soon as he did this, the girl began walking backwards, sweeping the ground in front of him with the branch. Ben followed her dutifully, wondering how far she had had to go to find the green leaves.

As they passed through the human tunnel, the stamping seemed to make the ground move and Ben could feel his spirits lifting in response. Part of him wanted to stamp too, to shout until his fear flew away. He looked back at his mum, who seemed to sense Ben's courage was growing. She smiled, urging him onwards.

At the end of the tunnel, just inside the gap in the fence, stood Senteu with two much older people, a man and a woman, all of them holding beaded collars like the ones the young people were wearing. Ben felt his legs turn to jelly. This was it, but he had no idea how to move forward.

Then suddenly, by some miracle, he found himself standing in front of them, not knowing how he had got there, nor how Kip had come to be by his side. He stared at his grandparents and they gazed back, their corrugated faces pouring out love towards him. Tears filled the old lady's eyes, and when she reached out to touch Ben's face, she smiled and the tears tipped over and streamed down her beautiful dark cheeks. It was almost too much, and Ben was grateful when Kip reminded him to bow his head before them.

'Benedict Olmoran!' said Ben's uncle solemnly. 'My name is Senteu Lemeikoki Olmoran. I am your father's brother. You are welcome.'

Senteu placed his hand upon Ben's head. Had he really just used the word *welcome*? wondered Ben, shivering slightly.

Then the collar his uncle had been holding was

fixed around Ben's neck. The beads attached to it fell down into his field of vision, trembling as they hung there.

'Benedict Olmoran!' continued Senteu. 'This is your grandfather, Koipapi Saitoti Olmoran.'

The hand upon his head this time was warm and heavy and full of power. And as Ben's grandfather placed another beaded collar over the first, Ben felt like he was being knighted by a king.

'And this,' said Senteu, 'is your grandmother, Koko Tikako Olegilisho.'

Her hand felt much lighter, but was just as warm, and Ben could have happily stood underneath it for a lot longer. Then as the final collar of beads was draped around his neck, the singing became much louder and Ben looked up to see all the young people pouring into the *manyatta* to form a ring around him and the adults.

Kip stepped backwards to become part of the outer circle. As their eyes met, he jutted his chin in the direction of their grandfather. Ben glanced at Koipapi just in time to see him being handed something that looked like a small baseball bat.

The old man lifted the gourd to his mouth and

took a long drink from its contents. The singing got louder. Ben braced himself. He turned to face his grandfather, who took two steps towards him and sprayed him with the liquid he had held in his mouth. It smelt sweet and was immediately sticky on his skin. This action was repeated two more times, then his grandmother ululated loudly and that was it. The ceremony seemed to have come to an end.

CHAPTER 9

Kip hugged him, his mum hugged him, and then just as Ben was trying to remember what came next, his grandmother grabbed him by the hand and led him towards one of the mud huts. Ben tried to calm himself with the thought that he had just been spat on by his grandfather, so a cup of tea with his granny should be a walk in the park.

As he followed her lead, he noticed the ground under his feet was soft and springy, like thick moss. 'It's poo, bro!' said Kip, jogging to catch up with him. 'Cow dung – the most comfortable thing you'll ever sleep on.'

Ben stopped in his tracks.

'Just kidding!' laughed Kip. 'You should see your face. We don't really sleep on it. We use it for a lot of other stuff, though – like building houses.'

They arrived at the little hut and Ben's grandmother stopped and stroked his face again, smiling so broadly that her eyes almost disappeared. Then she invited Ben's mother to enter the hut first, before beckoning Ben and Kip to follow.

'Feel this!' said Kip, stroking the outside wall proudly. 'It could pour down on this house and it wouldn't spring a single leak. Don't know why everyone calls them mud huts – we should call them poo huts.'

Ben liked his cousin more and more, but couldn't get his head round the way he sounded like a TV presenter and looked like a cave dweller.

'Right,' Kip continued, gesturing towards the doorway, 'let's not keep Granny Koko waiting.'

The entrance to the hut was without an actual door, but there was a little wall to walk around, presumably to keep the wind out. Once inside, the first things that greeted Ben were absolute darkness and extreme heat. He stood on the threshold, afraid to move, in case he stood on something or someone. Then, as his eyes became used to the lack of light, he discovered the source of the heat – a tiny fireplace in the centre of the room. He was grateful to see his mother's blonde hair glowing dimly in the darkness, like a torch with low batteries. She was sitting on a very tiny stool against the opposite wall, which indicated the limits of the room – two strides wide and about three or four long.

Granny Koko was crouching by the fireplace, watching over an old enamel kettle. She spoke to the boys in a language Ben didn't know, but he somehow understood exactly what she was saying, and they both sat down obediently on two little stools at the women's feet.

Milky tea was poured slowly into a chipped tin mug and passed to Ben. The idea of it was not incredibly appealing, but the taste was something else: warm, sweet and strangely fruity, not at all like tea at home. He took another sip, and then another. It occurred to him that on a boiling hot day like this, in an extremely warm room such as this one, a cup of tea might normally push him over the edge, but not now. It was all so cosy. He could feel his muscles beginning to soften like molten wax, and all his worries were melting away. If he stayed in here much longer, he might even start dribbling.

'Hey!' whispered Kip. 'Stop hogging the tea! Give it back to Koko!'

Ben did so, and she beamed at him, gently stroking his face yet again with her warm, leathery hand. Then she refilled the mug and passed it to Ben's mum, who took a few sips and passed it back. Granny Koko filled it again, took a drink, then passed it to Kip. This cycle was repeated several times, with no one saying anything, and Ben felt like he could easily fall asleep right where he was.

Eventually, the comfortable silence was broken by the entrance of Koipapi and Senteu, who crouched down at the fireplace and were handed the tea mug immediately. After taking several draughts each, they exchanged a few words with Granny Koko, then got up and left. Koko looked at Kip.

'*Keo enkiringo*,' she said, and Kip leapt to his feet.

'The meat is ready,' he said to Ben, 'and you are to have the first piece. Let's go!'

After Ben's eyes had readjusted to the bright sunlight outside, he noticed that there were animals everywhere – cows, sheep, goats. Where had they come from?

'These are your cows,' said Kip. 'But we don't have time to chat to them now, you can meet them later. Let's eat first, I'm starving.'

In the centre of the *manyatta* there was a fire in a big metal pan, like an oversized wok, on the ground. And over the top of it hung a makeshift barbecue with several pieces of meat sizzling away. Ben realized with enormous relief that this was the last part of the ceremony Kip had spoken about. He was almost there.

As Kip drew nearer, his grandfather took a sharp stick and speared a piece of the meat, then passed it to Ben. The finish line was in sight.

Kip had taught him how to say '*ashe oleng*', which meant 'thank you' in the Maa language, and he said it now whilst taking the meat. There were many nods of approval.

He recognized the taste of steak immediately, and though it was a bit tough, it was incredibly flavoursome. Everyone watched him with great anticipation as he chewed and swallowed.

'Delicious!' he pronounced with feeling. Kip translated and everyone laughed. He was immediately offered more, which he ate with gusto. Then Koipapi said something in Maa, and Kip's face fell.

'What did he say?' asked Ben, through a mouthful of meat.

'He says you have a good appetite,' replied Kip under his breath suddenly. 'Like your father.'

Koipapi gave some sort of command to the other elders, who nodded and turned their attention to the cows around them. They were searching for something. Ben looked to Kip for an explanation, but his eyes were fixed on the ground.

Suddenly there was a flurry of activity as a brown cow was selected from the herd and dragged forward by its horns. It mooed in protest and Ben noticed how the other cows moved out of the way quickly as though they were used to it. A gourd and a bow and arrow were handed to Koipapi, and Ben's blood ran cold as he realized what was happening. Why hadn't Kip mentioned this?

One elder took the cow's head and pulled it up and to the side, presenting its neck. Koipapi crouched down with the agility of a man much younger than his obvious years. His entire focus was on a vein that was now bulging from the animal's neck, which he touched gently with a practised finger. Then, taking the bow and arrow, he lined them up at point blank range and, with absolute precision, pierced the chosen vein.

Ben's whole body flushed hot and then cold, as though he had suddenly woken up to find himself teetering on the edge of a cliff. As his grandfather brought the gourd up to collect the blood, which was now pouring from the cow's neck, the world around Ben began to spin. Despite the heat of the sun, Ben's arms and legs were beginning to freeze and he was rapidly losing all feeling in his face.

His grandfather closed the wound in the cow's neck with something that looked like mud, then stood up and began walking towards Ben. He stopped in front of him, lifted the bottle of blood to his lips and took a drink which seemed to last a lifetime. Then all Ben's fears were realized as the gourd was passed to him.

He made a feeble attempt to reach for it, determined not to fail, but his hands kept missing. He swung round to look for his mum, but his head felt like it was made of marble all of a sudden. Unable to hold up its weight any longer, he sank to the ground.

CHAPTER 10

Ben stared at the canvas ceiling of his tent. There was a faint tapping noise coming from his mum's laptop as she worked outside on the veranda. He was supposed to be resting, but his brain was buzzing way too fast for that.

So, it had finally happened – the thing he feared most, the thing his mum had warned him about – but for some reason it wasn't as bad as he'd thought it would be. When his cousin had pulled him up off the floor, everyone seemed to carry on as normal. There were no shocked faces, no derisive laughter. Someone had offered him some more meat, but his granny elbowed them out of the way and tried to make him lie down in her hut. It was almost as if they had expected this to happen. Eventually, Kate had persuaded them that it was probably best for him to go back to the camp and rest, so Trevor came to collect him in one of the safari cars.

The tapping noise stopped. Ben wondered what his mum had been writing about, and suddenly he remembered the letters she had hidden from him.

'How you doing?' she asked suddenly, her face obscuring his view of the ceiling.

'What time is it?' he croaked.

'It's about four o'clock. You OK?'

'Yeah. Kind of.'

'What's wrong?'

Ben said nothing.

'Come on, sweetie, we tell each other everything, remember?'

'Not *quite* everything, though, Mum, is it?'

'What do you mean?'

'Why did you never mention the letters that Kipat and Granny Koko wrote?'

His mum exhaled loudly, and her shoulders drooped as if the balloon holding her up had just burst.

'I was wondering when those particular chickens

would come home to roost.' She looked at him guiltily. 'Ben, I'm so sorry, you must feel hurt.'

'Yeah, but I don't understand why you didn't tell me about them.'

'You really want to know?'

'YES!'

She took a deep breath. 'I didn't want to lose you.'

'What do you mean?'

She looked up at the ceiling and bit her bottom lip. 'Well, Ben, you see, your father was my soulmate. We'd not been together very long, but we were going to get married.'

'Yeah, you've told me that before,' he said.

'I know, but it was a surprise to *us* at the time. I didn't believe in fluffy romance, and he was from a completely different culture, where wives are important because they're useful. He could have had several if he wanted.'

Ben couldn't really see what this had to do with the letters.

'But when we met, something different happened. It was like there was some outside force bringing us together. I hadn't told your father I was pregnant, Ben, but as he lay dying in my arms, he said, "Look after our baby."'

It was clear to Ben that she was trying not to cry, perhaps for his sake, but it was no use. She shut her eyes as if trying to gather strength, and the tears tumbled out.

'There was something so meant-to-be about us,' she said. 'I still don't understand why he died.' She gave a few sobs before drawing breath to speak again. 'I'm sorry, Ben, I've been so selfish. I was scared of coming back because I knew there would be reminders every-where of the love I lost. I kept the letters from you because I didn't want to lose you too.'

'But why would you lose *me*?'

'Oh, Ben, if it hasn't already hooked you, it will. Give it time.'

'What?'

'Kenya, my darling – everyone who comes to Kenya, falls in love with it! Especially the Maasai Mara. And for you, well, it's in your blood.' She dabbed her runny nose on the back of her hand, catching sight of her watch as she did so. 'Yikes! I have to get ready for our first shoot. We've had a tip-off about poacher activity tonight, and we want to try and intercept them.'

'Really?'

'Yes, there's a strong chance the poachers are planning to take one of the elephants we saw yesterday. We might be able to catch them in the act.'

'Can I come?'

'Ben, we've spoken about this. The poachers are armed with guns to bring down the elephants—'

'But what about you?'

'I'll be fine! We have bullet-proof vests, and there'll be two armed rangers with us who are well used to dealing with poachers. And Senteu will be there, of course, and he's more useful than everyone else put together. If there's a problem, we'll just press the record button and get out of the way.'

'But how can you expect me to stay here, knowing you're out there being shot at?'

'Ben! Your father told me to look after you, and I did warn you about this, didn't I?'

'OK,' he conceded, forlornly.

'Thank you.' She smiled and got up to go.

'Mum . . .'

'Yes, my love?'

'What's up with Senteu?'

'What do you mean?'

'He seems so cross, like he doesn't want us to be here or something.'

'No, I don't think it's that. But we probably bring back memories for him – things he doesn't want to remember.'

'Like what?'

'Well,' she paused, 'it's not easy losing your brother that young. And also . . .'

'Yeah?'

'Ah, Ben, can we talk about this tomorrow? I have to go and prepare the kit now. If you want to come and help me, Jez and Phil get ready, we'll be up in reception.' She kissed him on the head and turned to go, but then stopped again. 'Hello, Kipat,' she said brightly.

Ben sat up. His cousin was standing at the entrance to his tent, smiling right at Ben as though he was the centre of his universe.

'Hello, Auntie!' Kip said first, out of politeness. Then with much more exuberance, 'Hey, bro!'

'Hi,' said Ben, trying not to sound too flattered.

'Well, I'll leave you two to chat, then.' Ben's mum turned to leave, touching Kip's bowed head as she left.

'This tent is sick, man.'

'Yeah, it's cool,' said Ben, starting to get up.

'Hey, be careful! You should move slowly after fainting.'

'I'm fine!'

'That's 'cause you landed on cow dung. I told you it was comfortable, didn't I?'

'I'm so embarrassed!'

'Why?' asked Kip. 'We've all done it.'

'Yeah, right!'

'What, you think you're the only one who ever fainted at the sight of blood?'

'No, but I bet *you've* never done it!'

'And how would you know that? Did you ask me?'

Ben stared at him.

'Go on, ask me!'

'Have you ever fainted at the sight of blood?' asked Ben, mechanically.

'Yup. We all have. It runs in the family.'

'It . . . what?' Ben stuttered.

'That's right! Everyone's got it on Koipapi's side. We've just learnt how to control it.'

'Wait, so why didn't you tell me about that part of the ceremony?' Ben asked. 'You told me about every-thing else.'

'Yeah, I'm sorry about that, bro,' said Kip, looking slightly embarrassed for the first time. 'But Koipapi wanted to see if you really did have the family fear of blood.'

'So what now?'

'Well, that's what I came to tell you. The elders are meeting this afternoon to discuss it, and they'll tell you what they decide tomorrow.'

'Do you think they'll reject me?' asked Ben.

'Reject you?' exclaimed Kip. 'Er, well, let me see. Our prodigal son returns after thirteen years and proves that he really is one of us because he has the same blood phobia. Hmmm. Should we reject him? Well, maybe because he's an IDIOT! Of course they won't reject you.'

'Well, what *will* they do, then?' asked Ben, trying not to laugh.

'I think they'll be working out a way that you can overcome it and prove that you could become a warrior.'

'Wow! Do you know what it'll involve?'

'Could be anything, really. But let's just wait and see – you have cows to meet.'

'Cows! Where?' asked Ben, peering outside the tent.

'I thought you'd be a bit tired after falling face down in all that poo,' laughed Kip. 'So I brought them to you.'

CHAPTER 11

Up at reception, the atmosphere was charged with nervous excitement as Ben's mum and the film crew checked and double-checked their equipment before loading it on to the waiting Land Cruiser. In the distance, about a hundred metres from the front of the camp, Ben's cows were waiting under a tree. The gentle sound of mooing could be heard distinctly.

'Come on!' said Kip, pulling Ben by the elbow. 'Let's meet the herd.'

But Ben was rooted to the spot.

'Don't be scared,' said Kip. 'They're your inheritance.'

'It's not that.' Ben nodded in the direction of the Land Cruiser.

Two camouflaged rangers with very large rifles had just arrived. They shook hands with Senteu and Trevor before climbing up to take their places in the vehicle.

Although Ben had seen guns in films more times than he could count, he had never actually laid eyes on one for real. There was something solid and unforgiving about them, and it left him with a cold feeling in the pit of his stomach.

'Kipat!' called Kate. 'Will you keep an eye on Ben for me?'

'Mum!' groaned Ben.

'No problem!' Kip put an arm around his cousin. 'A warrior never leaves another warrior on his own.'

Kate and Senteu both suddenly turned and stared at Kip like he was a ghost. He cleared his throat and swung his arms back and forth self-consciously.

'Thank you, Kip,' said Kate, glancing at Senteu, who turned back to the Land Cruiser like a gathering thundercloud.

'Mama Benedict?' asked Kip, in a quieter voice.

'Yes, Kipat?'

'Please can I take Ben to meet his cows?' He pointed to the thorn tree in the distance where the beasts had gathered.

'Yes, of course,' she said. 'But it will be dark in a couple of hours. Please don't stay out after that.' After she had hugged Ben and said, 'Bye, I love you, be good!' a total of three times, she piled into the Land Cruiser with the rest of the crew and drove away.

'Come on,' said Kip. 'Let's do this!'

They wandered over to the thorn tree to meet the herd. Ben thought he recognized a few of the cows from earlier, including the one who had given blood.

'You're right, bro,' said Kip, stroking the brown cow. 'This is Ayah, you can see where the wound has been sealed. You know your cows, man, you *must* be a real Maasai.' Ben tried not to beam. He felt a bit sick at the memory of the bloodletting, though, so that helped him keep a straight face.

One by one, each cow was introduced to him. 'Look into their eyes!' Kip suggested. 'When you really see who they are, whisper something lovely in their ears.'

'Is it all right if I just stroke them to start with?' He'd never been this close to a cow before, never mind actually spoken to one.

'Sure! Do you want to help me take them back

home? Are you feeling strong enough?'

'I feel fine, but I don't think I could find my way back on my own, and Mum will kill me if I'm out after dark.'

'Well,' said Kip, 'what time is it now?' He reached under his toga and pulled out a small phone.

'Hey!' said Ben. 'I've got the same phone as you!'

'Best phone for the bush, bro – always got reception and the battery lasts for ever. Smartphones are a waste of time here.'

Ben could feel his face warming as he thought about how ungrateful he'd been; he was glad his cousin was looking at the phone and not at him.

'Oh, we've got plenty of time,' Kip concluded, stuffing his phone back into its hiding place. 'I'll get you back for seven-thirty, that's just half an hour of real darkness. I'm sure your mum'll be fine with that.'

The journey to the village was so much more enjoyable this time. The cousins talked without stopping, as though they were trying to fit the last thirteen years into half an hour. The sun setting over the ridge made everything look so peaceful, and a feeling of completeness began to rest upon Ben, like this was just where he was meant to be.

They rounded the brow of the hill that overlooked the *manyatta*, pausing there to gaze at the sunset whilst the cows broke into a canter down the hill towards their familiar resting place.

Ben put his foot on a large boulder by his side and stretched gently. He was just about to change to the other foot when Kip suddenly pushed him off balance.

'Quick! Get down behind that rock!' his cousin gasped.

Ben did so, partly because he had no choice, having already been given a hefty shove. He thought Kip was playing a game with him, and was just about to complain about it when he caught sight of his face. Kip was staring, panic-stricken, at something at the bottom of the hill.

Ben peered round the other side of the giant stone which was partly covered by a thick bush. He could just see through it enough to make out a dirty-grey empty pickup truck parked outside the entrance to the *manyatta*.

'Who is it?' asked Ben, feeling completely bewildered.

'I can't tell you right now – you're just going to have to trust me. Stay here, and don't move or go anywhere until they've gone. And above all else, don't let them see you.' Kip was speaking with his jaw tightly set like a ventriloquist, and when Ben looked back down the hill again he could see why.

Three men in T-shirts and khaki trousers had just come out of the *manyatta* and were standing by the pickup, staring up at Kip. One of them had a rifle, and another was holding a long metal bar. They didn't look like rangers, and they definitely weren't Maasai. Ben's heart started to race.

'Laters, bro!' Kip whispered, as if this happened every day, and began walking down the hill. When he was within two strides of the men, he stopped and bowed his head, but something told Ben these men wouldn't reach out to touch it as he had seen the Maasai elders do. And he was right.

The man without a weapon got into the driver's seat of the vehicle. Kip walked past the others and into the *manyatta*. They followed him, looking over their shoulders and scanning the horizon as they went.

After a while, Ben wished he'd brought his phone so he could tell how long he'd been crouching down behind the boulder with his eyes fixed on the pickup. He could feel himself beginning to shake uncontrollably, which just added to his sense of uselessness.

Perhaps he should run back to the lodge and get help, he thought; maybe one of the lodge staff could do something.

Then suddenly Kip screamed from somewhere inside the *manyatta*, and the man in the driver's seat of the pickup turned on the engine. A few moments later, the other two came running out. One of them was carrying the metal bar which he threw into the back of the truck – Ben heard it clatter as it made contact. Then both men jumped in after it, and had barely landed before the driver set off, alarmingly quickly, in the direction of Ben's boulder.

The vehicle slowed down as it climbed the hill, and though Ben's heart was almost pounding out of his ears, he was well hidden and could get a good look at the men as they drove closer. The two in the back had sat down on opposite sides of the truck and were holding on to the rail running around the outside of the cab. The man who'd carried the metal bar wore a red-brown T-shirt, the colour of dried blood, which looked as though it hadn't been washed in weeks. The man with the rifle was similarly scruffy-looking, but his shirt had no sleeves and, as he passed by, there was a scar visible on his upper arm in the shape of an upside-down V. Just as Ben was trying to remember where he had seen this before, the first man rose to his feet, banged on the top of the cab and stared back in Ben's direction.

The pickup stopped immediately, and the armed man raised his rifle. Ben's stomach turned cold, and he tried to squash further down into the bush without giving away his position. But the truck clunked into reverse and began moving slowly backwards.

As it drew closer, the man in the dark red T-shirt bent over, scanning the bush and boulder for signs of life. Ben could see that his face was horribly disfigured as though he had been burnt, leaving one side of his mouth turned up in a permanent half-smile. His eyes, though, were laser beams, and Ben could feel his insides turning to liquid as he realized the inevitability of being discovered.

The truck stopped just a few metres away, the engine ticked over and Ben felt like he might pass out. Then suddenly there was a rustling sound at his feet, and a rabbit shot out from the bush, ran in front of the pickup and was off over the open plateau.

The gunman pointed at it and laughed, then he mimed being scared of the rabbit and shooting it as it ran. Ben couldn't help but think he might regret this later, if the expression on the disfigured man's face was anything to go by, but after the gunman had mocked his companion to his full satisfaction, he shouted down to the driver in a language Ben didn't recognize, and they moved off at speed.

And despite the cloud of dust that was left behind, Ben could see the man in the blood-red shirt staring fixedly in his direction until he was out of sight.

CHAPTER 12

Ben burst into Granny Koko's house – it was the first place he could think of where Kip might be. Sure enough, Kip was sitting on the ground, hugging his knees with his head resting on his arms. The embers of the fire were scattered about and the little stools had been knocked over, like a whirlwind had passed through the house.

'Kip!' panted Ben. 'You OK? What happened? Who were those men?'

'Those men, cuz, are poachers.' He looked up at Ben and smiled, but the smile was forced, and it gave Ben a chill.

'What did they do to you?'

'Can you help me untie Koko and Grandpapi, please?' It was like he was asking for help with the washing-up or something.

Ben looked around the tiny, dark room. He hadn't noticed the bed that lay behind a sort of curtain last time he was in here, but there it was – a basic frame with animal skins on top, and his grandparents tied to each leg.

He lunged towards Koko and fumbled around with the knotted rope until it gave way. She began a steady stream of Maa, as though freeing her hands had released her voice as well. She stroked Ben's face, then knelt down to unbind her husband, reaching behind him to the leg of the bed he had been tied to. An upside-down V had been burnt into it, looking like it had just missed Grandpapi, who seemed completely unfazed by everything. Koko touched the mark and then turned to Kip, her words becoming faster and more passionate.

He tried to push her away gently, but she was un-deterred and seemed to be working herself up into a frenzy. Ben wanted to yell at them, make her stop, ask them what had just happened. Then Koipapi put a gentle hand on Koko's arm and spoke two or three words in Maa; she stopped shouting but continued with a low continuous muttering.

'Come on, Ben,' said Kip, sounding strangely upbeat. 'Let's get you back to the lodge.'

He followed Kip out of the hut and tried to smile at his grandparents as he went. It seemed like a pathetic gesture, but what else could he do? He couldn't talk to them.

They secured the animals in their pens, then walked out of the *manyatta* and up the hill in silence, until Ben couldn't stand it any more. 'Kip,' he said, stopping in his tracks, 'what happened in there? I heard you scream – are you all right?'

'We have to keep walking, bro, it's getting dark.'

Ben walked on a few paces and then stopped again. 'No. I'm not going anywhere until you tell me what happened.'

Kip sighed. 'All right, but keep walking, OK?' Ben jogged to catch up with him as he walked on ahead. 'The poachers are a gang. They have control over the area, and they like to keep us quiet.'

'Quiet about what?'

'Who they are. Where they are. They know why your mother's here, and they came to remind us to keep our mouths shut.'

'Do they know *I'm* here?' Ben asked quietly.

'No. And they don't know that your mum and my dad are related, either.' He paused. 'It's probably best not to mention that you saw the poachers with me, bro.'

'Why?'

''Cause your mum might not trust my dad any more.'

'OK. So what was the mark on the bed all about?'

'It's a cattle brand. Anything that belongs to them gets branded.'

'Yeah, I think I saw the scar on one of them as they passed.'

Kip stopped. 'They didn't see you, did they?'

'No,' Ben said. 'But it was a close call. Kip, why did you scream?'

'Because Shetani, their leader, was about to brand my face.'

'Oh my God!' Ben could almost feel the searing pain of it on his own skin. 'So why did they brand the bed instead?'

'To show how hot it was? To leave a calling card for my dad? To scare the living crap out of me? They said it would be me next time. They always do stuff like that. It's a big performance.'

'Which one is Shetani?' Ben asked, already knowing the answer.

'The ugly one in the red-brown shirt. Shetani means *devil*, and he's that all right.'

Ben shuddered, remembering the eyes that had bored into him as he'd tried to hide. He'd never been so scared in his entire life.

'Are there only three of them? I'd always imagined there'd be loads more.'

'There's about six in total. They don't like to get too big, 'cause then they'd run more of a risk of being shopped.'

'To the police?'

'Not exactly! There's no 911 here, or 999 or whatever it is. The police come later. It's the park rangers that they fear first, and people like your mum – people with international power.'

The boys pushed on up the path, keen to reach the lodge before dark. They were nearly at the top of the hill now.

'I was surprised to see Shetani here today, though,' said Kip. 'He's like the Godfather – never shows up for the dirty work unless he has to. He must be worried about what your mum's up to . . . Ben, please don't tell my dad that you heard me scream.'

'Why?'

'Warriors are not meant to show fear or pain. He'll say I'm not ready to become a man. Hopefully Grandpapi won't tell him either.'

'If I was about to be branded, I'd scream the house down.'

Kip smiled, and the heavy weight that seemed to be pressing on him appeared to lift a little. And just as Ben was about to smile back, he tripped over something and fell to the ground.

'Man, the floor is your friend today,' said Kip, offering him a hand to pull him up.

'Wait a minute!' said Ben. 'What's that?' He pointed to a long, dark shape that lay across the path.

'What the . . .?' Kip jumped back and peered at the thick tubular object through the deepening gloom. He fumbled for his phone and turned on the torch setting. At least the phone had that, Ben noted.

'*Ngai!*' Kip exclaimed. 'I thought it was a snake. It's not a snake, is it? I hate snakes.'

'It looks like . . . an elephant's trunk,' whispered Ben.

'It *is* an elephant's trunk!' Both boys took a step backwards. Ben suddenly thought he might throw up.

He glanced at his cousin, who didn't look any better.

'Where's the rest of it?' Kip shone the torch around the surrounding area, which revealed nothing but roots and bushes, and Ben followed the beam of light with his eyes – more out of concern for lurking poachers than bits of elephant. He had known in his bones that Shetani wasn't convinced by the rabbit. So maybe this was a trap . . .

'What's this?' asked Kip, bringing Ben's attention back to the trunk.

Kip stretched down and gingerly plucked a piece of paper from the nostrils of the severed trunk.

'Is that writing?' asked Ben, straining to look as Kip unfolded the note. 'Well?'

'Ben, this is meant for your mother. It's from the poachers.'

'What does it say?' Ben's heart was pounding.

'It says if she doesn't get her nose out of their business . . .'

'What?'

Kip was silent.

'What?' urged Ben. 'What does it say?'

'It says they'll kill her, but—'

'Oh my God! Are you sure? Let me see.'

'Yes, but—'

Ben grabbed the note. 'Oh my God!'

'Ben! They're just trying to scare her. Your mum'll be fine.'

'How do *you* know?'

'Because she's with my dad. She's completely safe, I promise.'

'But your dad doesn't have a gun. *They* have a gun. Didn't you see it?' Ben's voice was wavering, and he knew it would turn into tears if he carried on.

'But the rangers have guns,' said Kip. 'Listen, bro, my dad screwed up once before, there's no way he's going to let anything happen to your mum as well.'

'What are you talking about?'

Kip wrinkled his brow. 'Don't you know?'

'About what?'

'Hasn't your mum told you how your dad died?'

'Of course – the lion . . .'

'Yeah, but—' Kip put his hand on Ben's arm. 'Bro, you're shaking like a newborn lamb.'

It was true. He had tried not to show it, but he just couldn't hide it any more. Everything seemed to have got to him suddenly.

'Let's go inside,' said Kip. 'Surum, the head barman,

makes a fat hot chocolate.'

'W-what do I do with the note?' Ben was holding it aloft like he was waving a white flag.

'I guess we'd better give it to your mum. But remember not to tell her you saw the poachers.'

'And the trunk?'

'The hyenas will deal with that. It'll be gone by morning.'

CHAPTER 13

The boys sat at the bar, hunched over four mugs of cocoa, like two little old men. About halfway through the first cup, Ben had stopped shaking. Now he was on to his second, he wasn't in such a hurry and could just enjoy the intense sweetness of it, without anyone telling him he'd had enough.

'Good huh?' said Surum the barman, smiling at the boys. They both nodded in agreement. 'Let me know if you want another, OK?' The boys looked at each other in disbelief. Surely three was illegal.

'So,' said Kip returning to the conversation they'd been having outside, 'you said that you know your dad was killed by a lion?'

Ben nodded. 'He was protecting Mum and the crew.'

'And the only reason the lion could attack him was because he was on his own. Did you know that?'

'What do you mean? The film crew were there.'

'But he was the only *warrior*, and a warrior should never be on his own.' Kip gazed into his cocoa. 'My dad was meant to be with him.'

'So why wasn't he there?'

'Granny Koko says that our dads weren't just brothers, they were best friends, but when your mum came along, they stopped spending time together. Basically, my dad was jealous and stayed home that night to teach your dad a lesson.'

'What for? Being with my mum? Some lesson!' Ben pushed his hot chocolate away, unfinished.

'Well, it's not like he *meant* for your dad to die, is it?'

'So why is *he* angry with *me*?' Ben hissed. 'Should be the other way around.'

'Bro! He's not angry with you. He's ashamed of himself. Did you know I've never seen him smile? Granny Koko says he used to smile all the time before your dad died. That's why we wrote to your mum – we wanted you to come here so Dad could see his brother lives on in you. Then maybe he'd smile again.'

Ben sighed. 'Well, he certainly hasn't smiled at *me*.'

'Listen, Ben, I don't want you to feel sorry for him, I just want you to know that your mum is safe. Because he'd do anything not to let it happen again.'

It was about eight-thirty by the time Ben joined the others at breakfast the next morning, and several minutes later before he could get a word in edgeways.

'How did we miss them?' Ben's mum said, her head cradled in her hands.

'We'd probably have got there in time if the Land Cruiser hadn't conked out,' said Trevor. 'I'm sorry about that.'

'Well, these things happen, and at least we had Senteu there to fix it.'

'Yes, but it took him far too long. We lost a lot of time there.'

'I just don't understand why they took the trunk,' said Phil, pushing bacon and eggs round his plate. 'They won't get any money for it.'

'Indeed! It's very strange,' Trevor agreed. 'Certainly never happened before.'

'Mum . . . I think I know what happened.'

Everyone stopped trying to eat and stared at Ben.

'Morning, darling! What do you mean?'

'Well, Kip and I were walking back from the *manyatta* and we tripped over an elephant's trunk on the path leading up to the lodge.'

All the eyes on him widened.

'And it had this note with it.' He passed the dirty piece of paper to his mum. Jez, Phil and Trevor shot to their feet and huddled round her to get a closer look.

'Darling, that must have been awful. Was there a lot of blood? Did you pass out?'

'It was pretty horrible actually, but I'm fine now.'

'So you must have been out after dark, then?'

'Well not exactly, it was *nearly* dark, about quarter past seven.'

'You didn't see the poachers, did you?'

'No!' He played with some sugar crystals on the tablecloth, wishing everyone would stop looking at him.

'Well, don't go out after dark again tonight, will you?'

'But I *wasn't* out after dark. And why are we talking about me? You're the one with the death threat.'

'Oh, don't worry about that!' she said, casting the note aside. 'I've had them before. Wait a minute, though – what did you do with the trunk?'

'We left it out there, where we found it – just past the tree. Kip said the hyenas would take it.'

'He was right,' said Trevor. 'I've already done a perimeter walk and there's nothing there.'

'Excuse me,' said the camp receptionist, appearing at the table suddenly. 'There is an elder here to see you and your son.'

'Ah, that must be your grandfather,' said Ben's mum, attempting to be cheerful. 'Come on!' They pushed back their chairs and went to find Koipapi and Kip, under the thorn tree.

Ben bowed his head before his grandfather and Kip did the same to Kate. 'Mama Benedict,' said Kip, 'Grandpapi would like to talk to you, but he has asked me to translate. Is that OK?'

'Of course!' She smiled warmly at Koipapi, who immediately began to speak in Maa.

'Grandpapi says,' said Kip, 'that the elders have decided what to do about Ben.'

'Oh?' said Kate.

Ben realized they hadn't talked about this yesterday, what with her going off for the night shoot so quickly. She looked a little left out suddenly, and Ben felt awkward for her.

'The elders say,' Kip continued, 'that it is time for Ben to do battle with his fear of blood. If he is a real Maasai, he will win.'

Ben looked at Kip, who shrugged apologetically. Koipapi continued, his gaze fixed on the horizon, his expression inscrutable.

'Grandpapi says that Ben must go on a seven-day journey with me, to complete seven challenges . . . leaving this afternoon.'

'Go where?' asked his mum.

Koipapi gave a broad sweep of his arm in reply.

'What?' she gasped. 'The bush? Oh, no. There are men with guns out there, not to mention lions.'

'Koipapi says he will go too,' Kip said. 'He will guide us and give the challenges.' Kip paused to let his grand-father speak again. 'And he says that the men with guns are looking for elephants, not Ben.'

The boys glanced at each other, then looked away again quickly.

'I'm sorry,' said Ben's mum, her voice rising in pitch, 'but this is ridiculous!' She began to move away.

'Stop!' said Koipapi firmly, and she did – but prob-ably because of his sudden use of English as much as anything else. The look on her face as she turned was not an expression of someone who was giving in.

Koipapi raised his chin in the direction of the boys, and they both knew immediately to move away. As they walked, Kip whipped out his phone from under his toga.

'Right,' he concluded, 'I'm giving him five minutes to convince her.'

'How's he going to do that without you?'

'He speaks a little bit of English, and your mum speaks some Maa. They'll manage.'

'OK, but you don't want to be on the wrong side of her in an argument. She might look all soft and gentle but she's a beast in a debate. She'll crush you!'

'Ben, our grandfather was one of the bravest warriors ever,' said Kip. 'And did you notice the amulet of blue beads on his forearm? That shows he is the wisest of all elders. If he can't convince her, no one can.'

'So, what if he does?' asked Ben. 'It's not like I can go, is it?'

'Why not?'

'What, you think I should just go off and leave Mum behind when there are psycho poachers out to kill her?'

'And how exactly do you plan to help with that?'

Ben could feel his hands tightening into fists at his side.

'Listen, bro, it's true what I said about my dad – he won't let her come to any harm – but don't you want to learn how to take care of her yourself? You need to beat your own fear first, then you might actually be of some use to her.'

Just when Ben thought he wouldn't be able to hold back any longer from giving Kip a punch in the eye, his mum stormed past them in the direction of her tent, looking like she was about to explode. Kip checked the time on his phone and nodded. He hugged Ben before he could protest, then ran off to join his grandfather.

Ben's mum was lying face down on her bed, crying weakly into her pillow, when he caught up with her.

'Mum,' he said gently, 'are you OK?'

'Oh, Ben.' Her voice sounded strangled. 'Sorry about all these tears. Ever since I started yesterday, I can't seem to stop.'

Ben felt the urge to hug her again, which was pretty weird, as he was normally trying to fight off her hugs. 'What did Koipapi say?'

'Just that I'm a terrible mother,' she spluttered. 'That I have to stop protecting you, and that *you* must learn to look after *me*. He said that if I don't let you go on this seven-day challenge thing, you'll never become a man and you'll always hate me for it.'

Ben wanted to protest, but after what Kip had said, he couldn't help feeling there might be something in it.

'He also said I had to tell you about your uncle Senteu.'

'If it's about how Dad died, I already know.'

'What? How?'

'Kip told me last night.'

'Oh, Ben, I'm sorry. You must be angry.'

'Kind of. I just don't know why *you* didn't tell me. You always said we didn't have any secrets, but it turns out that's not true. Are there any more?'

She shook her head. 'No more secrets, Ben. I didn't tell you about Senteu because I wanted to give him the freedom to tell you himself. I forgave him a long time ago, but he's never been able to forgive himself.'

Ben let out a big sigh.

'A lot's happened in the last two days, hasn't it?' his mum said, sitting up and wiping her eyes. He nodded slowly in agreement.

'I'm very sorry that I kept you from your family for so long, my love. I'm absolutely furious with your grandfather, but I think it's because I know he's right. So, all that said, what would *you* like to do?'

Ben looked at her tear-stained face and felt something inside him let go. Everyone always seemed to be telling him what to do, except her. She was the only one who'd ever asked him what *he* wanted. Yes, she'd kept the letters from him, but only because she was scared.

Then suddenly, and before he was even aware of having made the decision, he wrapped his arms around her and held her tightly against his chest. The poachers dropped into his mind, and he pulled her closer as he remembered their terrifying faces. He didn't know which was more frightening – the poachers he'd seen or the lions he hadn't. And both were out there. But he was tired of feeling like a weakling, like someone who never amounted to anything. Perhaps this was his only chance to do something about it.

'What was that for?' Kate asked, when he finally let her go.

'Just thought I'd give you a taste of your own medicine.'

'More, please!'

'Mum,' said Ben, ignoring her plea. 'I get it that you want to protect me, but I think Koipapi might be right and I need to accept the challenge.'

'Yes!' she said. 'That's my boy!'

'But he's not right about everything, you know.'

'Why do you say that?'

'Well, you're not a terrible mum, are you?'

'Oh, Ben,' she said, looking like she was going to cry again.

'And don't worry, I'll be fine. After all, how hard can these challenges be?'

CHAPTER 14

B en glanced back over his shoulder. Uncle Senteu and Ben's mum were now just stick figures in the distance – one standing straight and stiff, the other waving exuberantly.

'Bye darling,' his mum called, her light voice lifted by the wind. 'Good luck!'

To see him off, she had worn her bright red lucky trainers, and had promised not to take them off until he returned safely. Now she shook them in the air, one at a time, like a crazy elf.

'Love your mum's trainers, man,' said Kip.

'Uh, sorry, she gets a bit excited sometimes.'

'What? If I had a pair of red Reebok Classics, I'd

be shaking them around too.'

Ben looked back again and waved briefly. Ever since he'd decided to take up his grandfather's offer, his mum had been racing around, filling his backpack with sun cream, fruit and water, only to be told that it all had to be left behind. In the end, she'd hidden the sun cream, his phone and a small bottle of water on the carrier donkey when Koipapi wasn't looking.

His grandfather had insisted that he wear the same traditional clothing as Kip, but Ben hadn't expected Senteu to be the one who would dress him. Ben had stood quietly in just his shorts and trainers – the only items of his own he was allowed to keep – whilst his uncle draped him with a thin red blanket, tying it like a toga at the shoulder, then securing it with a belt at the waist. Finally he was wrapped up in another, thicker blanket called a *shuka*. And despite Senteu's total lack of expression, there was something about the way he attended to the smallest details of Ben's clothing that made him think he wasn't doing it unwillingly.

Ben tried to catch his eye, to elicit a smile, but perhaps it was too early for that. So, although he was stiflingly hot, he decided to keep the *shuka* on – just as his uncle had arranged it – until they were well on their way and Senteu was out of sight.

The first challenge of seven was cattle herding. Of course, Kip already knew this skill inside out, but his job was to teach Ben.

Koipapi was leading the way, a few hundred metres in front, picking his way slowly through the rocky escarpment and down to the plain that stretched out before them like an enormous patchwork quilt. There were different tones of olive and beige, dotted here and there with acacia trees and it was all sewn together with the lush greenery that mapped the course of the Mara river.

They negotiated their way down the rocky slope as Kip sang a melody that sounded slightly sad to Ben, but he noticed that the cows had stopped mooing – almost as if they were listening. When the boys finally reached the bottom, they looked up to find Koipapi hadn't even paused for breath and was still a good distance in front of them, presumably aiming for the river.

Ben wondered if this would be his grandfather's default position for the entire trip. There were so many questions he wanted to ask about his father, but the old man was just so hard to reach.

'Right!' said Kip suddenly. 'The first thing a Maasai must learn about his cattle is how to love them.'

'Love them?' Ben stifled a laugh and it came out as a snort.

'I'm serious, man, you have to love your cattle, they're a blessing from Ngai.' Kip looked like some sort of Scottish gangster in his red tartan *shuka*, but his message of cow-love was making it difficult for Ben to take him as seriously as he seemed to want.

'The song I was just singing is a very old love song. You need to learn that song, bro, so your cows *know* you love them.'

'But I can't sing,' replied Ben, thinking this was probably the least of his worries.

'It doesn't matter. They need to know the sound of your voice so you can soothe them when they're stressed. If they're calm, they won't stampede. And believe me, you don't want a stampede.'

'I need a drink,' said Ben, keen to change the subject as much as anything else. He caught up with the carrier donkey and looked for his phone tucked into the panniers. There were already two messages from his mum and he'd only been gone an hour or so.

He cast off his *shuka* at last and pulled out the small, illicit bottle of water, then unscrewed the top and took a long drink.

'What are you doing?' cried Kip, after whistling at the cows to stop. 'Don't drink so much. You have to pace yourself, man.'

Ben paused mid-drink.

'And you need to turn off your phone too – the battery won't last for ever!'

Ben had not seen this side of his cousin yet and it gave him a sinking feeling. They had seven whole days together – the last thing he needed was an obsessive bossy-boots, especially when his only other companion was a silent old man.

As he returned the water to the donkey bags, his hand touched the bottle of sun cream. In all the madness of their departure, he hadn't put any on, and he could bet that at least one of those text messages was reminding him of that. Oh, well, it would be a shame to have to return early because of sunburn. He flipped open the lid.

'What do you need that for?' said Kip.

'I don't want to get burnt.'

'But your skin is built for the sun, bro. You're a Maasai.'

Ben carried on applying the cream, pretending he hadn't heard.

'Stop it!' shouted Kip. 'Do you want to smell like someone from another planet? All the animals will run away, including your cows. You need to smell like them, or you'll freak them out!'

'But *you* don't smell like a cow!'

'Yeah, but I don't smell like Nivea factor 30 either, and that's why they love me!'

Ben opened his mouth to speak, but nothing came out.

'Now, if you've finished,' said Kip gruffly, 'you'd better learn how to herd or Grandpapi will be on my case.'

Ben took as long as was humanly possible to put the sun cream away.

'Right, bro, you will notice that the cows are now eating. They will do this any chance you give them. So, if you want them to stop grazing and get going, you whistle at them like this.' Kip made a sound like a hyperactive blackbird, and the cows immediately responded by walking off. 'Right, your turn now.'

'But they're already moving,' said Ben.

'Just give it a go!'

Ben did the best impression he could muster of Kip's manic whistle, and the cows immediately stopped moving forward, put their heads down and started eating grass. 'Was that supposed to happen?'

'Yes!' said Kip, excitedly. 'It's the same command for stop and go!'

'Well, that's easy.'

'Exactly! Now, you get them going again and then I'll show you the commands for left and right.'

Ben got the hang of it all pretty quickly, and actually enjoyed it a lot more than he'd thought he would. So much so, in fact, he hadn't noticed that Kip had stopped herding altogether, leaving him in control, until he saw Koipapi waiting for them in the trees.

He glanced over his shoulder to see that Kip had pulled right back. Ben felt immediately stupid for getting so uptight about the sun cream and threw his cousin a cheesy grin by way of an apology. Kip winked back, and the air was clear again.

As they neared the trees, the cows picked up their pace, eventually plunging their noses into the lush green grass that had not yet been scorched by the baking sun. Like animals that had been starved for months, they tore up great mouthfuls of it, over and over. Koipapi and Kip both took up the same position as they watched the herd – leaning on a stick, standing on one leg, a slight smile spread across their faces. Ben wanted to try it himself, but thought he'd probably fall over, so he squashed the idea and just stared at the cows instead, trying not to look too awkward.

As the quiet set in, Ben realized that something was bothering him, and the stillness seemed to be drawing it to the surface.

'Kip,' he said softly, 'what happened to your mum?'

'She died – giving birth to me.'

'I'm sorry, that's sad.'

'No more than you and your dad, bro.'

'So your dad lost his brother *and* his wife.'

'Dad thinks Ngai was punishing him for abandoning his brother.'

'That doesn't seem fair.'

'No. The only things he has to live for now, are me and the cows. And the cows are actually yours, so . . .'

'Kip, I don't understand why the cows belong to me.'

'Your dad was the firstborn, what more can I say?'

Kip looked at Ben as if he was expecting some kind of response. 'OK, bro, do you really not have any idea what I'm talking about?'

Ben shook his head.

'Well, when a Maasai gets to a certain age, like Grandpapi, he gives his cows to his firstborn son. If the firstborn son dies, all the cows go to *his* firstborn son. If there is no firstborn son of the firstborn son, the cows go to the second-born son.' Kip looked at Ben meaningfully. Ben stared back. 'You still don't get it, do you?'

'Not really.'

'*You're* the firstborn son of the firstborn son, so all the cows are yours.'

'Oh!' exclaimed Ben, catching on at last.

'Did you not take tea this morning?' said Kip. 'Your brain is like a slug.'

'It feels like a slug – must be the heat. But wait, I haven't even been here for the last thirteen years, so why didn't Koipapi just give them to your dad?'

'Ngai said you would come for them, bro. And here you are.'

'That must have been really hard for your dad.'

Kip nodded and pursed his lips.

'So, why've *you* been so cool about it?' asked Ben. 'With me, I mean. The cows would be yours if I wasn't around.'

'You're family Ben. If we take care of our family, everything else takes care of itself.'

'Thank you.'

Kip smiled.

CHAPTER 15

Without a word from anyone, the cows began to move through the trees and down to the river to drink. But Ben hung back. He could see thick bushes and very long grass – there could be anything hiding in there . . .

'Come on, cuz,' said Kip, not even bothering to look back. 'No lions here!'

How did Kip know what he was thinking all the time? Maybe it was a family superpower – in which case, perhaps Ben had it too. It would be a cool upside to having to put up with the blood phobia. Whatever it was, Ben decided it might be better to go for the 'safety in numbers' option, and followed at a semi-trot.

Before the boys had even reached the river's edge, the smell of cool, fresh water rose to meet them. Ben's thirst awoke immediately, reminding him it was far from satisfied. He wobbled his way across three large rocks, almost falling in a couple of times, then stretched down into the water, cupping his hands to scoop it into his dry mouth.

'No!' shouted Kip. 'The water's not clean, it has to be boiled.' He pointed towards Koipapi, who was kneeling in a clearing some distance from the river and blowing into what looked like a pile of twigs on the ground. A thin, steady stream of smoke was starting to rise into the air. 'When the cows have drunk, we'll take milk. That'll give your thirst a kicking.'

Ben couldn't think of anything less likely to quench his thirst right now than milk, but there was always the remaining water in the bottle on the carrier donkey. Maybe he could find a way of sneaking over to it.

When the cows had finished drinking, they were herded back up the riverbank. As Ben was watching them move, Kip grabbed his hand, nearly making him jump out of his skin.

'You need to find the one with the biggest bag,' said Kip, following the cows to their patch of grass.

'Bag of what?' asked Ben, trying in vain to pull his hand away.

'Milk, of course!'

Kip chose his cow quickly and then bent over to take a closer look, pulling Ben over with him. Try as he might, Ben couldn't seem to yank his hand away. It was bad enough that his mum and granny kept doing this, but his cousin – not OK! Then, as if he was trying to wind him up, Kip began moving Ben's hand over the cow's hindquarters, all the time drawing closer to her udders.

'I thought we were supposed to be training to be warriors,' said Ben gruffly, 'not milkmaids.'

But then Kip silenced him by moving his hand on to the udder itself. It was surprisingly soft and squidgy, like a big stress ball. The cow stamped her foot, and Ben instinctively pulled his hand away, but Kip held it there, steady.

'She's just kicking away the flies,' said Kip. 'Don't worry, she wants you to do this.'

Ben looked at his cousin – he was actually serious.

'So, first,' said Kip, 'you choose one of the teats and grasp it lightly, then squeeze like a wave from the top down.'

Koipapi suddenly appeared at the other side of the cow and placed a wooden bowl underneath. With perfect timing, a gentle spray of white liquid hit the bowl. Kip remained with his hand on top of Ben's for three more squeezes, then let go.

'I think you've got it now. Carry on,' he instructed.

Ben continued squeezing but the milk stopped. The cow kicked again, definitely in annoyance this time.

'Urgh,' said Ben in frustration.

'No, bro! You have to stay calm. There's a song you sing to a mother cow when you want to take her milk.'

'Of course there is!' mumbled Ben.

'And remember, gentle squeezes from top to bottom, don't just yank the thing!'

Kip stood up and began to sing, walking to the front of the cow and kissing her face, as far as Ben could make out from the sounds.

Ben tried again. Nothing. Then suddenly Kip's hands were on his shoulders, gently pushing them down.

'Relax, bro!'

Ben hadn't realized he wasn't.

'And breathe,' said Kip, laughing at him softly.

Ben let out a loud exhalation and a perfect jet of

milk squirted into the bowl, making him let go in surprise.

'Keep going,' said Kip pressing Ben's shoulders down again. 'You have to fill that bowl.' He resumed his singing, wandering through the cows like he was weaving a milking spell.

Ben took up the position again, dropped his shoulders and reminded himself to breathe. In no time at all the sound changed from milk thinly spraying the bottom of the bowl, to that of liquid powerfully shooting into liquid. He stopped and stared at the perfect white pool for a moment.

'It's full,' he said slightly under his breath. Then, bouncing to his feet in triumph, 'It's full, Kip, the bowl is full!'

'Er, no, it's not,' said Kip.

Ben looked back at the bowl. The cow must have kicked it over – he knew she didn't like him.

'First rule of milking, bro: take the bowl with you when you get up.'

'*Now* what are we going to do?' moaned Ben.

'Oh, well, I don't know, cuz, where do *you* think we're going to get milk from in the middle of nowhere at this time of day?' He pretended to look around him and then did a cartoon double take. 'Huh? Who put all those cows there?'

Ben couldn't decide which was more annoying – bossy Kip or smug, sarcastic Kip.

Eventually they picked another cow with a 'big bag' and filled the bowl again with her milk, lifting it out of the way quickly this time. Ben carried it proudly back to his grandfather, who characteristically said nothing, but held out a gourd. It took Ben a few moments to realize he meant for him to the pour the milk into it. Why didn't he just say so? He couldn't help but shake a little as he attempted to pour the milk from the wide container into the narrow opening, and it seemed like most of the liquid spilt on to his grandfather's feet. He didn't seem to mind, though, and some of it must have hit the target because Koipapi took a long drink from the gourd before passing it on. Ben's skin prickled at the memory of his last experience with such a thing, but he took a tentative sip nevertheless.

The liquid was warm and incredibly creamy, and once he took his first sip, he found it difficult to stop. But then the flavour caught up with his thirst, slamming the brakes on immediately. He pulled the gourd from his lips and passed it to Kip, but the taste of cow was pulsating in his mouth, as though he'd actually licked one of the animals and then been kicked for the insult. His stomach lurched towards his mouth briefly, and as the gourd came back round to him again, he politely declined.

When the milk was finished, they all lay in the grass to rest whilst the cows munched around them, some of them lying down too. Ben stretched his hands behind his head and gazed at the cobalt sky that was broken into shards by the branches of the trees.

'Kip,' said Ben, 'do you really have to protect the cattle from lions?'

'Er, yeah,' he replied, looking at Ben like he had gone completely mad.

'Do they ever eat people?'

'Who, the cows?'

'Ha, ha!' said Ben, without laughing.

'It's very rare. Lion prefer the taste of livestock.' Kip glanced at Ben. He was picking at the grass, over and over. 'I don't blame you for being scared.' He lowered his voice. 'Keep it to yourself, but I'm shit-scared of lions too.'

'Really?

'Yeah. Anyway, you're lucky.'

'How?'

'Your dad was killed by one.'

'I'd hardly call that lucky.'

'Ah, so you don't know?'

'What?'

'When a Maasai is killed by a lion, he takes on the animal's spirit. Grandpapi tells me that the lion who killed your father was found dead soon afterwards.'

Ben looked at him blankly.

'It gave its spirit to your dad, and now you can't come to any harm, 'cause your dad is watching over you with the spirit of Simba.'

'That's ridiculous!'

'Why?'

'It sounds like the Lion King.'

'Well, where do you think Disney got it from? And anyway, you know what they say about clichés.'

'What?' asked Ben.

'A cliché is only a cliché 'cause it's true.'

'How do you even know that word?'

'That's very patronizing.'

'Whatever!'

'Seriously though,' said Kip, 'don't you talk to your dad?'

Ben shook his head.

'You should, especially when you feel scared. But anyway, Ngai helps those who help themselves, so after we've had a rest, we'll build a *boma* out of thorn bushes. That'll keep out our furry yellow friends.'

CHAPTER 16

Kip was true to his word, and they spent the rest of the day cutting and gathering thorn bushes to make a cattle pen.

'Pass me that *simi*, will you?' said Kip, pointing at a wooden handle that was sticking out of one of the panniers.

'Whoa!' said Ben as he pulled it out, not expecting there to be a large blade shaped like the head of a spear on the other end of the handle.

'Oh, yeah,' laughed Kip. 'Don't suppose you have those in London.'

'Not really.' Ben passed it to Kip at arm's length.

'The *simi* is your friend, bro – it's good for

everything. Watch this!' And Kip made short work of hacking a shrub to the ground. 'In English, this bush is called a "wait-a-bit", 'cause its thorns are so fierce that when they get you, you have to wait a bit for someone to come and help.' Kip chuckled to himself.

The whole process took about two hours, by which time Ben's arms and legs were stinging and burning all over. As he looked closer, he could see they'd been shredded by the thorns. At least now he understood why a lion might think twice before trying to push its way through.

'Right!' said Kip, shutting the last animal inside the *boma*. 'You get that bag off the donkey, and we'll go and make supper.'

This was not as easy as it sounded, but once Ben had managed to corner the animal and take off its bags, it gave him the perfect opportunity to have a drink of water and check his phone. There were three messages from his mum now – the first two didn't really say anything – *blah blah, sun cream, blah blah* – but the third was different. *Off on our second night shoot. So excited! Sure we'll get them this time.*

Ben went hot and cold. But what had he thought would happen? She was hardly going to stay in the camp the whole time, sitting in her tent with her lucky trainers on.

Kip called him over towards the fire.

'You all right?' he asked, as Ben drew near.

Ben nodded. He didn't want to tell Kip about the message – he knew what he would say: 'She'll be fine, she's with my dad.' And whether he was right or not, Ben would just have to believe that for now – what else could he do?

'Well,' said Kip, 'whatever it is, some food will make you feel better. Come on!'

Kip joined his grandfather and crouched down by the fire. They were both annoyingly good at that – perfectly balanced, with their feet flat on the floor, like Yoda and his grandson. Try as he might, Ben just couldn't do it without feeling like he was going to topple over, either forwards into the fire or backwards with his feet in the air. So he played it safe and just sat down on his backside.

It reminded him of the time his other grandfather had taken him fishing with his cousins in Scotland – they'd all sat on their 'shooting sticks' but Ben hadn't had the first idea what to do with one. If someone had just explained that you had to unfold the top bit of leather and then counterbalance your weight against it, it would have been so much easier, but nobody did, and he was way too embarrassed to ask.

Koipapi handed him a strip of dried meat and a bowl of hot soup. Ben was so hungry, he didn't hesitate to tackle the meat, but he hadn't expected it to be so fatty. Just as he thought he might have to spit it out, Kip made a loud slurping noise.

'You gotta try the soup, bro! You can't have one without the other.'

He was right – its herby warmth seemed to melt away the congealed fat that was clinging to Ben's teeth and gums, leaving his mouth feeling instantly cleaner.

'Told you!' said Kip without looking up.

Night fell within half an hour, or so it seemed. It was so quick that Ben felt caught out somehow, like he wasn't quite ready for it yet.

Koipapi stoked up the fire and Ben watched him, wondering if he was ever going to mention whether they had passed today's challenge or not. Until at last he turned and spoke to Kip in Maa and Ben waited for the translation.

'Grandpapi has given the next challenge,' said Kip eventually. 'Tomorrow you must face your fear of blood!'

Then their grandfather lay down on the ground, pulled his *shuka* over his head and started snoring.

Night-time in the Mara, Ben quickly discovered, was deafening. Insects, birds, frogs, not to mention Koipapi's snoring.

The boys didn't speak for a while – Ben didn't know what to say or do. How was he supposed to just overcome his fear of blood? If he knew how to do that, then he wouldn't be here, would he? He needed help and had no idea where to find it in the middle of the African bush.

'Any ideas?' asked Kip, after Koipapi had been snoring for a while.

'Sadly not,' said Ben. 'You?'

'Yes, I do,' he said, 'but it's all about using your imagination. The fear of blood is not like other phobias 'cause it makes your blood pressure drop, not rise, so you faint.'

Kip sounded like a medical journal. Where had he learnt all this, Ben wondered?

'So,' Kip continued, 'you have to keep your blood pressure high by using your imagination.'

'And how on earth do you do that?' asked Ben.

'Easy!' Kip reached under his toga and produced a small, smooth stone. Ben made a mental note to ask him where he kept everything.

'Whenever there is a blood situation,' said Kip, 'I think about a beautiful girl from a *manyatta* near ours. Then I stroke this little stone and imagine it's her bottom. Here, you try.'

'I don't think that's going to work,' said Ben.

'Why not?'

'I don't know the girl you're talking about.'

'Yeah, 'cause that's *my* girl. Get your own girl!'

'Still not going to work.'

'Why?'

'I can't think of a single girl whose bottom I want to stroke.'

'Oh!' said Kip. 'Well, my dad says he gets angry and that works for him.'

Why am I not surprised? thought Ben.

'What makes *you* mad?' asked Kip.

'I dunno,' said Ben. 'Maybe the whole blood thing – that makes me a bit cross. Like, why do I have to have it? It's so embarrassing.'

'A bit cross?' exclaimed Kip. 'Embarrassing? I'm talking about your insides boiling and your eyeballs popping out.'

Ben could feel Kip staring at him in the darkness, waiting for some kind of response.

His mum was always saying he looked angry, even when he wasn't. She had this really annoying habit of ironing out his brow with her fingers. He wondered what she was up to now, and his thoughts automatically turned to the dirty-grey pickup. In his mind's eye, he could see Shetani holding his mum captive in the back, grinning while she tried to get free. A new surge of adrenaline entered his bloodstream, and he could feel his jaw beginning to set tight.

'You've got it, haven't you?' asked Kip. 'I would not want to be the person you are mad with right now. You should see your face.'

'I thought of someone hurting my mum,' whispered Ben, careful not to mention the poachers specifically, for fear that Kip would start going on about his dad again.

'Nice!'

'Not really.'

'Well, whatever works, you know what I mean? So, when you're faced with the red stuff, that's what you need to do. Close your eyes and bring all that back to mind. The more detailed the pictures, the better. Got it?'

'Er, I think so.'

'Right, we need to get some sleep,' said Kip, throwing some more wood on the fire.

'But it's so early!'

'Doesn't matter, bro! In the bush, you follow the sun – lie down with it and rise with it too. Are you not tired? You've done a lot: you built a *boma*, milked a cow, passed your first challenge.'

'I did?'

'Yup!'

'But Koipapi didn't say anything, I thought—'

'Our Grandpapi is a man of few words.'

'Well, come to think of it, I *am* quite tired.'

'Exactly! Well, get in here, then,' said Kip, holding up his *shuka*.

'Sorry, what?'

'You've never done this before, have you?'

Ben froze. He didn't really want to think about what 'this' might be.

'Right, so I'll spoon you tonight, then tomorrow night we can change over.'

'Er, I think I'm all right, thanks.'

'Aw, come on, this is how the warriors do it. You'll get cold if you lie on your own.'

'I'm fine,' said Ben. 'Really!'

'Well suit yourself, but you'll have to keep the fire going. That's the rule for he who chooses to sleep alone.'

Then Kip put his *shuka* over his head, just like Koipapi, lay down and went to sleep.

CHAPTER 17

~~~~~~~~~~~~~~~~~~~

Ben didn't realize he'd fallen asleep until he felt Kip tugging at his foot. He tried to yank it away, but Kip just made a growling noise in response and pulled really hard on his trainer.

'Get off!' groaned Ben. 'It can't be time to get up yet.'

Kip growled again. *This is ridiculous*, thought Ben. *Maybe he's cold, but who steals a sleeping man's shoes?*

'I'm serious,' said Ben. 'Get off!'

It took one more growl for Ben to realize that it didn't really sound like his cousin at all. In fact, it sounded more like a dog...

Suddenly, Ben was wide awake. He looked down at

his foot. There was a hyena attached to it. A HYENA!

His brain flooded with information that he streamed and filtered with digital speed. Hyenas *were* dogs, he knew this from his mum's wildlife films. It was much bigger in real life, and it stank.

The questions followed with equal velocity – was it him or the shoe it wanted? Why was Kip still asleep? Where was Koipapi?

Oh my God, thought Ben, *perhaps this thing has eaten my grandfather.* And then he couldn't hold it in any longer. He screamed.

The hyena let go but immediately others came to join it – grunting, barking, whooping. The noise was hideous, like a choir of cackling hags.

Mixed in with the rising racket was the sound of the cows beginning to stir. Their lowing became more intense and the sound of their hooves on the ground quickened. Ben could feel their energy rising to panic. How could Kip sleep through this?

He SAS-crawled over to his cousin and shook him awake, but it was too late. The cows had started pushing against the thorn bush barrier; finally it gave way, and they burst through in all directions. Several of them charged towards Kip and Ben, looming out of the darkness like bovine ghosts, forcing them to dive for cover.

Then suddenly Koipapi was there, trying to head the animals off, whistling and grunting at them, desperate to contain them. But it was no use. The whole thing must have lasted less than two minutes, but every animal had vanished. Every cow, donkey, goat and hyena – gone!

The day was dawning and the light seemed to grow as quickly as it had fallen, making it possible to see more clearly at last. But what Ben saw made him wish for the darkness to come again. The cow pen was completely destroyed. Pieces of thorn bush were scattered everywhere. All their hard work was ruined.

Ben watched as Koipapi spoke to Kip briefly in a low voice, then walked off in pursuit of the herd.

'Ben,' said Kip, 'Grandpapi says you should stay here and rebuild the fence. We're going to try and get the animals back.'

Ben opened his hands in front of him, appealing to Kip for some explanation.

'Sorry, bro,' his cousin said. 'But that's why you need to sing to your cows.' Then he turned on his heels and was off at a jog, following their grandfather.

Ben watched Kip and Koipapi walk away until he couldn't see them any more. He thought they'd said a warrior should never be alone.

But then, he wasn't a warrior, was he?

A lump of guilt was hardening in the pit of his gut; he shouldn't have screamed. But doesn't everyone do that when they're being dragged off by a wild animal?

He scanned the debris strewn on the ground and located his bag immediately. He could see his phone poking out of the top. He hesitated. If he really wanted to show his mum he could take care of her, then he could hardly ask her to come and rescue him.

Just then, the phone flashed and vibrated briefly as if saying hello. *Great night!* said the text message. *We intercepted a kill. Poachers got away but we saved an elephant! How was day one? Love, Mum.*

Ben's stomach turned cold.

How could she be so upbeat? If she'd stopped the poachers from getting their ivory, wouldn't they be more ready than ever to . . .? He couldn't even think about it.

He looked again at the scattered remains of the camp. The *simi* lay in the middle of the mess, glinting hopefully. Ben ran to it and grasped the wooden handle – just holding it gave him confidence. If a lion attacked him, at least he could defend himself.

But perhaps he *should* rebuild the fence; if he was going to die, then he might as well do something to pass the time.

He took a deep breath and began by gathering what still remained of the carefully cut and constructed fence, then laid it out in a vague approximation of the previous structure. There were enormous gaps – the cows must have dragged the bushes with them as they went – but thankfully the thorn bushes seemed to be growing in abundance around here. He grasped the first one gently, trying to avoid its sharp barbs, but as he grew in skill and confidence he began to choose the more aggressive-looking ones, working faster and harder all the time, driven onwards by the thought that his grandfather must surely be proud of him now.

CHAPTER 18

When he had built a cattle pen that was higher and stronger than the first, Ben lay down in the centre of it, thirsty, hungry, covered in scratches but satisfied. *They might never come back for me*, he thought to himself. *I might die here, but I have made this thing.* He chuckled to himself, then laughed out loud. He had no idea why the thought was so funny, but he laughed harder and harder until, suddenly, his laugh sounded a bit like a moo.

He stopped and listened. And there was the moo again, but it seemed to be coming from some bushes about fifty metres away.

He jumped up and crept as quietly as he could

towards it, quickly breaking into a jog, anxious not to lose the only remaining cow. And as he neared the bush, the cow's noises became louder and more intense, like it was in pain.

If Kip was here, he'd probably sing his ridiculous song. Ben hadn't been able to get it out of his head since yesterday, but he couldn't remember the words. Maybe he should try humming it – after all, what did he have to lose?

At first, it came out as a few dry croaks and Ben felt stupid, like it might actually be Kip behind the bush and at any minute he'd jump out and say, 'Fooled you!' But as Ben found his voice, the painful sounds of mooing completely stopped.

He peered round the bush. It was one of their cows all right, but something was wrong. Her head was down low, and every so often she would swing it from side to side, trying to bite her flanks. She gave a long, low moo as if she was asking Ben for help, and he wondered if her back legs might be stuck in the thorn bush.

He reached out to stroke her neck, then ran his hand along her back like he'd seen Kip do. Then steadily, he inched round to her rear end and immediately froze at the sight of a tiny and very slimy little hoof, sticking out of her back end. So, she wasn't stuck in the bush, but it might have been easier for Ben if she was.

As his brain caught up with his eyes, the cow mooed again and bit at her sides, then gave a huge push. She shifted her legs and tried to brace herself, but nothing happened. Ben wondered if he should help her somehow. He started singing again, but slightly more nervously this time.

A video he'd once seen at school came to mind, about vets helping animals give birth. He had remembered being grossed out by it, but sadly that was *all* he could remember. He did know, though, that if he was going to help, he needed to be in the right place, and so he moved round to stand behind the labouring animal, all the while humming Kip's song.

Tentatively, he touched the little foot – it wasn't moving. He shuddered. Maybe this would make his task easier, but he hoped it didn't mean the calf was dead. He held his breath and closed his hands around the hoof. It was warm and wet. He let go as if he'd just been electrocuted.

The cow mooed again and gave another huge heave, but the hoof didn't budge.

Ben took a deep breath and grasped the tiny foot

again, grimacing at the feeling of it. It was almost too much to bear, and he was just about to let go when it all started again. Ben braced himself as the cow bit at her flanks and when she pushed, he tried to pull. But the hoof was too slippery and his hand flew off, almost hitting him in the face at the same time.

Instinctively, he took a corner of his *shuka* and wrapped his hand in it. He was just in time. The next push came around much faster – the warning signal first, then another powerful heave. Ben leant back, using his weight as well as his muscles to pull, but the calf's leg barely moved at all. There was something blocking it.

A flash of the video came back to him. He remembered when the vet had practically put his whole arm inside a cow and everyone in the class had screamed. He shuddered to think what his classmates in London would think of him standing here contemplating doing the same. But where to start?

He touched the hoof again, just holding his hand there for a few seconds, trying to drum up some courage. Then, very slowly, he explored a little further inside the cow, just under the protruding hoof. To his enormous relief, the problem was immediately obvious. Of course! One of the calf's other hooves must be catching inside.

With the one hand wrapped in his *shuka*, he grabbed the hoof he could see, then hooked the fingers of his other hand under the one that was stuck. Then it came – the mooing, the biting, the push. He lifted with one hand and pulled with the other. But nothing could have prepared him for what happened next.

Ben's manoeuvre had an immediate effect as both hooves catapulted towards him. But the release brought with it a massive explosion of blood. All over his face.

He turned away, trying to block it all out, but he could feel the fluid dripping down his neck and chest. And the smell! Repulsively sweet, like warm honey. Ben retched and fumbled for his *shuka*, then dragged the scratchy woollen cloth over his skin, wiping off as much of the gunge as possible.

The calf's front hooves were both out now. Its nose was also visible, and there were long, globular strings of dark red blood hanging down to the ground. Ben clamped his eyes shut and supressed another retch.

What was it Kip had said? The more detail, the better...

Swaying slightly but keeping his eyes tightly shut, Ben brought his mum to mind. She immediately looked scared, and although it felt wrong, he invited the poachers into the picture too, allowing them to hold her at gunpoint. Then his imagination took over and the men began jabbing their rifles in his mum's face and shouting, making her whimper and cry. Ben's anger shot up to boiling point, taking his blood pressure with it.

His eyes snapped open, and he was instantly aware that his reality had changed – the ground felt more solid, his muscles were taut. He was no longer a weak person. It had worked.

Desperate to turn his anger into action, he grabbed the calf's hooves. His timing was perfect, for as he pulled, the expectant mother gave one last push and the entire calf slithered out on to the ground.

Ben staggered slightly, then fixed his gaze on the slimy, calf-shaped sack lying motionless in a pool of blood on the ground. Why wasn't it moving?

He stared at the bloody calf, his hands balling up into tight fists. Had all this been for nothing? His mum was in mortal danger, his new family had abandoned him, and now there was a dead calf at his feet.

Just as Ben was beginning to wonder if the nightmare could get any worse, the cow turned around to examine the product of her labour. She gently nudged the inanimate sack and licked at the film that was covering her dead baby. Eventually this broke, and she began to clean all around the calf's face. She paid close attention to its nose, her pale tongue working its way deep into the nostrils.

Her optimism was killing Ben, and he wanted to scream at her to stop. Couldn't she see that the calf was dead? Then suddenly it seemed like there were two tongues . . .

Ben craned his neck forwards. Was the calf moving? Then, as if in answer to his question, it lifted its head from the ground and sneezed, releasing two big, floppy ears from inside the birth bag. And the mother carried on, cleaning and nudging until the tiny calf rose to a sitting position, very wobbly, but most certainly alive.

Ben's anger fell away as quickly as it had erupted, and he dropped to his knees, as if his fury had been the only thing holding him up.

The cow took two unsteady steps towards him, stretching out her great, wide nose towards his face, sniffing and breathing on him with her warm, soupy breath. He leant away from her but she tracked him with her snout and then just as he thought he could go no further without falling over, she gently licked his face.

'Hey!' said Ben. '*I'm* not your baby.' He tried to push her away. But she persisted, as though trying to say *thank you*, so he let her carry on, despite the fact that her tongue felt like sandpaper.

Ben looked at the calf, already making its first feeble attempts to stand and realized that he felt like it looked. He glanced down and saw that he was kneeling in a pool of blood – and yet he knew that he wasn't going to pass out.

'Benedict,' said Koipapi's voice, suddenly behind him. 'We go!' And his grandfather reached across him and picked up the calf.

'Go where?' asked Ben, looking up in surprise.

'Blood bring more hyena. We move!'

'But I made the cattle pen again. Look!' he said, pointing at his handiwork with a shaky finger.

'Now you make one more!'

And Ben's grandfather walked away, the newborn calf effortlessly slung across his shoulders.

CHAPTER 19

'Look at you, bro!' said Kip, genuinely impressed.

Ben wobbled slightly as he crouched down next to the milking cow, but he soon regained his composure and smiled at his cousin. Though his feet were not completely flat on the floor, he was already more stable than he had been two days ago.

'I'll leave it to the professional, then,' Kip said, and walked off to help Koipapi with the other animals.

As the old wooden bowl steadily filled with milk under his now more capable hands, it occurred to Ben that, for the first time in as long as he could remember, he felt good. The cow he'd helped yesterday was quietly grazing near him, her new calf nuzzling her for its own share of milk. It was like they trusted him. Even the cow in front of him was giving up her milk freely, as though she'd heard he was all right.

He rested his cheek on her warm flank. 'Don't fall asleep, cuz!' shouted Kip. Ben pretended to start snoring. He hadn't had a lot of sleep lately, though – it would be very easy to drift off for real. Last night, he'd been awake half the time worrying about his mum. Then in the morning, it had dawned on him that, if he had beaten his fear of blood, he could go home early. It was like a great weight had been lifted from his shoulders with the rising of the sun. Now he just couldn't wait to get back and make sure his mum was OK.

He patted the cow and rose to his feet, taking the bowl of milk with him. As he walked over to his grandfather and cousin, he noticed that the grass seemed greener. A gentle breeze stroked his skin, lifting his spirits and lending a lightness to his step. He poured the milk into the gourd, only spilling one or two drops, and then waited for his grandfather to take the first drink.

'Nice one,' said Kip.

Though Ben felt like he'd just sailed across the Atlantic Ocean single-handed and could have punched the air with delight, he just smiled smugly instead. 'So, what's the plan?' he asked. 'Are we going home now, or do we have to take down the cattle pen first?'

'Why would you want to do that? You built it three times yesterday; I've never built that many in one day in my whole life,' said Kip, handing the gourd back to Ben.

'Maybe we need to cover our tracks before we leave,' said Ben, between two long draughts of milk.

'I like your thinking, but we're not going anywhere yet. We have five more challenges to whack.'

'But I thought, now that I've beaten my fear of blood, we wouldn't need to bother with the rest.'

Kip glanced at their grandfather, then lowered his voice. 'Ben,' he said, 'you haven't beaten it yet.'

'What? But I told you what happened yesterday.'

Koipapi said something to Kip in Maa.

'He says you have only faced your fear,' said Kip, hesitantly, 'not *beaten* it.'

'What does that mean?' cried Ben. 'I *did* beat it. I booted it out of the park yesterday. How can he say that I didn't?'

Koipapi gestured towards the open plain that lay beyond the trees.

'Right, let's go,' said Kip. 'Challenge number three!' He reached for Ben's hand.

'No!' shouted Ben, pulling it away. 'I'm sick of this – everyone taking me by the hand and telling me what to do, like I'm a child. And talking in your language all the time, as though you're trying to hide something from me. No, I'll find my own way back, thanks.'

Kip let him walk on for a few strides before following. 'Come on, man, I didn't realize you don't like the hand thing. Maasai hold hands all the time. And I only speak to Koipapi in Maa so not to embarrass him – his English is really bad, bro!'

'It doesn't matter,' said Ben, waving Kip away. 'Just leave me alone.'

'Well, I would, but you're going the wrong way.'

Ben changed track.

'That's not right either.'

'Urgh! You always know best, don't you?'

'Well, I know my way home.'

Ben stopped. 'Which way is it then?' he barked, without looking round. He could hear the smile in Kip's voice and knew that, if they made eye contact, he would probably have to hit him.

'To your right. You should be heading for that hill

up there, the one that looks like a sleeping lion.'

Ben started walking again.

'But seriously, bro, there's actual lions out there and snakes – rats, even!'

'I don't care! I just need to get back to Mum.'

'Come on, I've told you, she'll be fine, she's with—'

'What? Your dad?' shouted Ben, whipping round like a spitting cobra. 'Is that the really scary one with the spear who is going to protect my mum against a load of men with AK47s?'

'Ben, just calm down, you don't understand—'

'No, YOU don't understand. She stopped the poachers from killing another elephant the night before last, so now they're going to be looking for her.'

'No, they're not.'

'How can you say that? Don't you remember the note? You must be completely insane. I should never have listened to you.'

'Ben, please, just trust me.'

'Why on earth should I trust you?'

'Because my dad is working for the poachers.'

The only sound for a moment was that of the plain winds blowing bravely through the atmosphere that crackled between the two boys.

'Your dad is one of *them*?' whispered Ben. The scar on Senteu's shoulder suddenly flashed into his mind. He knew he'd seen it somewhere before – how could he have been so stupid?

'No!' said Kip. 'Well, not exactly. They made it impossible for him to refuse. But his job is just to keep your mum away from them.'

'Oh, so he won't actually kill her himself. He leaves that up to them, I suppose?'

Kip sighed. 'No, man, you've got it all wrong. They won't kill her unless they have no other option. And they have another option.'

'But that doesn't mean she's safe, though, does it?'

'Ben, how many times do I have to tell you—'

'Yeah, yeah, she's with your dad, you keep saying that, but how can you be so sure?'

'Because if he doesn't keep her out the way, it's not her they'll kill.' Kip looked him straight in the eye. 'It's me.'

A shadow passed across his face. Suddenly he looked like an old man.

'What do you mean?' asked Ben. 'How do you know?'

'Because when they first came for my dad, Shetani held a gun to my head and said he would blow it off if Dad didn't do what they wanted. The other day was just a reminder.'

Ben stared at his cousin, and as he did so, a single fat tear fell from Kip's left eye. There were no other signs of emotion – no shaky voice or wobbly lip. Just one tear.

'Well, we should go back to London, then – me and Mum – so you're safe.'

'No!' exclaimed Kip, aggressively wiping the tear from his cheek. 'I knew you'd say that. That's why I didn't tell you earlier. You came here for a reason, didn't you?'

'Kind of.'

'So finish it!'

'But what about you?'

'What *about* me? The poachers have no idea where we are, and as long as we're at large, my dad can put his plan into action.'

'What plan?'

Kip grinned. 'He's going to lure the poachers into a trap.'

The two boys looked at each other.

'Does my mum know?' asked Ben, stunned.

'She does now. Dad said he'd tell her as soon as we left, then they could get started. The whole "save an elephant, let the poachers go free" thing, that's part of it – step one!'

It was like a swarm of butterflies had just been released from the bottom of Ben's stomach and were frantically fluttering upwards.

'Do you trust me now?' asked Kip.

The butterflies reached the top of Ben's head.

'Come on, bro,' Kip urged, 'this is your big chance to beat the fear. You can't give up now. Are you in?'

'S'pose so.'

Kip stepped forward, grinning widely, and pulled Ben into a bear hug that made him feel like his eyeballs might pop out.

'Get off!' said Ben, pushing him away.

'Ah, come on, don't tell me hugs are out as well?'

'Definitely! And don't ask me to spoon you again, bro, that's weird!'

'You just called me "bro"!'

'Whatever!'

CHAPTER 20

When they were well out of Koipapi's eyesight, Kip outlined his idea for the next challenge. 'Grandpapi says you have to make a bow and arrows and then show him you can shoot straight.'

'How the—'

'Don't panic,' said Kip. 'I have a plan.'

'Like father, like son,' said Ben.

'Ha! Good one!'

Kip fumbled around under his toga and pulled out a fairly sizeable and very sharp-looking knife. Ben was so confused now about where all this stuff was being stored. He had seen Kip without his *shuka* and there were no hidden pockets or anything.

'Where did you stash that?' said Ben.

'Never mind that now,' said Kip, 'We need to start looking for the perfect sapling for our bow.'

The next hour was spent paring, cutting and stringing a bow and three arrows, using various pieces of equipment found in the bush and under Kip's toga. When everything looked ready, Kip took his knife and cut into the thick trunk of a short, nondescript tree. It immediately oozed a dark, gluey substance.

One by one, Kip prodded the end of the three arrows into the wound, coating them with the sap and then rubbing that with a little dry soil. He manipulated the blob of resin in his hand, squeezing and shaping it each time, until it was no longer malleable and had set hard on the end of the arrow.

'Training arrows,' he said, proudly holding them aloft and regarding them from every angle.

Then Ben watched with admiration as Kip stretched the bow and fired the arrows, stretched and fired, stretched and fired, until he was satisfied that everything was ready.

'You want a go?' said Kip, offering the newly formed weapons to Ben.

'Well, I'd better, if I'm gonna pass the test, right?'

said Ben.

'Maybe not,' replied Kip. 'I was thinking, we want to get these challenges done and dusted ASAP, right?'

'Yeah.'

'And because it's going to take at least a day to teach you to shoot, I have a suggestion on how we can move straight to challenge number four,' said Kip, breaking the newly formed arrows over his leg.

As they neared the camp where Koipapi was waiting for them, Kip thrust the bow into Ben's hand.

'You carry this!' he said. 'Just hold it confidently and he won't suspect a thing.'

He walked ahead towards Koipapi, brandishing the broken arrows and talking excitedly in Maa.

Koipapi closely examined the pieces of arrow, then spoke to Kip in a hushed voice as though he was amazed.

'He's impressed, bro,' said Kip, winking at Ben. 'He says only a true Maasai can shoot training arrows with such precision and force that he actually breaks the shafts.'

The old man nodded to himself, then turned around and walked slowly back to the fire, around which their various bags and packages were kept. He searched amongst them, mumbling to himself in Maa.

Ben felt Kip freeze at his side. 'Oh, no!' he whispered. 'The old goat's brought his own.'

They both watched as Koipapi pulled out three arrows, just like the ones Kip had made and then broken. He ambled back towards the boys at an excruciatingly slow pace and offered the arrows to Ben.

Nobody moved or said anything for what felt like the longest time. Then, just as Ben thought he was going to be sick or burst into tears or possibly both at once, a blood-curdling scream came from his cousin.

'*SIAFU*!' he yelled, grabbing the bow from Ben's hand. 'KILLER ANTS!'

He thrashed the ground with the bow, over and over until it dangled, in several useless pieces from his hand. Ben did not need to look at the ground to realize there were no ants – for once, his grandfather's face told a very clear story.

There was only a couple of seconds' pause before Koipapi raised the arrows in the air. Kip sprinted off, escaping just in time before they made contact with his backside.

There followed a lot of shouting. Kip ran from bush

to bush with his grandfather chasing him and, although Ben couldn't understand a word, he didn't really need to, because it was like watching a cartoon. First Kip would attempt to placate his grandfather by creeping up to him apologetically, but each time he drew near, Koipapi tried to thrash him with the arrows and Kip would scream and run away. This happened several times, and just as Ben was wondering how on earth it was all going to come to an end, Kip slipped during one of his getaways and landed on a cactus.

Koipapi seemed to think this was the funniest thing he had ever seen, and immediately gave up trying to beat his grandson. He continued to laugh as he walked away and put the arrows back in the bags, and Ben wondered if his grandfather had ever really meant to beat Kip at all. Either way, he seemed to be quite satisfied with the outcome.

'Are you all right?' asked Ben.

'Oh, yeah, I'm fine,' said Kip, gingerly picking a cactus prickle out of his backside. 'Gets him every time, that trick.'

CHAPTER 21

Kip sidled to a position of safety behind Ben when he saw Koipapi coming back. This time, he was carrying a spear. Ben had spied it on the carrier donkey when they set out on day one, and had been wondering if and when it would be used.

All of the old man's humour seemed to have evaporated as he handed the spear to Kip and spoke to him in Maa. When he had finished, he turned and walked to a log a few strides away, sitting down upon it regally.

'What did he say?' asked Ben nervously.

'He said that you should be able to throw the spear further than me, because you're older.'

'Well, that makes sense, doesn't it?'

'Yeah, but he also said that because you're thirteen, if you're a real Maasai, you'll throw like a man. Like your father.'

'So? What's the big deal?'

'Bro, I like your attitude, but your dad was a legend with a spear . . . there's no way you can throw it as far as him.'

'Well, I can try.'

'No, bro, I don't think so. I've got a better idea.'

'Is it as good as the last one?'

'Hey! I was just trying to help.'

Ben raised his eyebrows.

'Listen! Here's what we'll do. You see those four gum trees over there?' said Kip, pointing to four straight trees that stood in a row, like line judges at an athletics meet. 'Well, if you treat that little bush just before them as the starting line, I reckon you can probably throw as far as the first tree.'

'That doesn't seem like a very long way.'

'Exactly! You go first and throw it as hard as you can. Then I'll just make sure my throw comes up shorter than yours. Got it?'

'It's worth a try!' said Ben, grabbing the spear and marching off towards the starting line.

'No!' shouted Koipapi abruptly from his log. 'Kipat first!'

Ben turned on his heel, walked back and handed the spear to Kip.

'OK, cuz,' whispered Kip. 'Plan B: I'll just throw it a very short distance. Grandpapi's as blind as a rhino anyway, he won't even notice.'

Kip walked up to a place a few strides back from the starting line, winked at Ben, then took his run-up. As he let go of his grandfather's spear, he made an exaggerated grunting noise, then fell over as if the extensive effort had wiped him out. The spear, on the other hand, had landed about six metres short of the first tree.

Koipapi shouted angrily at Kip and jabbed his finger in the direction of the second tree.

Kip's shoulders slumped. 'I guess he's not as blind as I thought,' he said under his breath.

'Not deaf neither!' shouted Koipapi, from his wooden throne.

Kip mouthed the word *sorry* to Ben then took another run-up with the spear. But this time it was Ben who made the noise, gasping slightly as his cousin released the weapon with an unexpected strength and grace. The spear landed with pinpoint accuracy at the distance of the second tree.

'Now Benedict!' said Koipapi, sternly. He was just like a Roman emperor, sitting there in his toga, deciding whether Ben lived or died.

As he walked out to the second tree to retrieve the spear, Ben felt all his confidence vanish like a vapour. His grandfather seemed to be deadly serious now, and his cousin looked as if he had lost all hope. What happened if he couldn't throw the spear 'like a man'? Was that the end of the whole thing? He realized he had not discussed the ground rules with anyone – did failing one challenge mean he'd flunked everything?

Ben grasped the wooden shaft of the spear and realized he had no idea how to hold it, never mind throw it. Both ends were finished off with a hefty piece of metal, one pointed, the other flattened but sharp as a razor. It was about five times as heavy as a javelin, and he had only ever *held* one of those – never actually thrown it.

As he walked back to the starting line, Ben attempted two different grips, but his amateur fumbling caused him to drop the weapon in the dirt.

'*Ngai!*' gasped Kip.

Ben glanced nervously at his grandfather. No reaction. Weren't grandfathers supposed to smile at you, give you sweets, take you fishing?

Ben took up position where his cousin had started – a few paces back from the starting line. But this felt ridiculously close, so he moved a little further back, holding the spear with both hands and stretching it up into the air as he had seen Olympic javelin throwers doing on the telly. The heavy metal end nearly pulled him over backwards, though, so he quickly tried to disguise his floundering by jabbing forward a few times with the other end.

When he had gathered himself, he glanced at his grandfather again, who, much to Ben's surprise, seemed to be smiling. The only other time Ben had seen this was at the welcoming ceremony, and quite suddenly it was as though his own father was sitting there, willing him on. But as Ben looked more closely, the smile disappeared – the Roman emperor had returned – and he looked ready to feed Ben to the lions again. He must have just been squinting in the sun, not smiling at all.

The whole episode had knocked the wind out of Ben. As he walked forward, holding the spear over his right shoulder, he could feel a perceptible tremor setting into his body. He would either have to give up and drop the spear or break into a run with it. He chose the latter.

Then – as if his body had responded to this decision with a gesture of gratitude – it took control.

The rhythm of Ben's run-up became steadily faster and faster, building in him a kind of power that he knew he didn't normally possess. And as his speed increased, time seemed to slow down. His mind emptied itself, and suddenly it was as though he was watching himself from the outside.

He observed his spear arm as it dropped down to his side and slightly behind him, then his left arm moved up in front of his face and pointed at the sky as if showing the spear where to go.

And lastly, with no conscious decision from Ben at all, his right arm shot forward and released the weapon into the air.

CHAPTER 22

The first thing Ben observed after letting go of the spear was that his grandfather had risen to his feet and was staring, transfixed, following the weapon's journey as it travelled through the air.

The next thing he noticed, immediately after the spear hit the ground, was the sudden heavy weight of Kip leaping on to his back.

'You did it, bro, you did it!' he yelled.

Much to Ben's amazement, not only had the spear soared past the second tree where Kip's throw had reached, but it had flown on past the third too, eventually giving in to gravity a fair distance beyond the fourth tree.

Ben stared.

If it was not for the ache throbbing in his right shoulder, there was no way he would have believed that the throw had been his. He looked to Koipapi, who nodded, turned on his heels and returned to the cows that were now scattered around the camp. Open-mouthed, Ben watched him go – why had he not said anything?

Kip, on the other hand, was doing a celebration dance – grunting and shuffling, pushing out a rhythm up to the left for two counts then down to the right for two. He moved around Ben in ever-decreasing circles until it became too hard to ignore him.

'Stop it!'

'Why?' asked Kip, in between victory chants. 'Go Ben! Go Ben!'

'Shut up!'

Kip stopped. 'What's wrong? You nailed it.'

'Koipapi doesn't think so.'

'I told you, bro, he's a man of few words. He'll let you know that you've done a good job, just when you need to hear it.'

'Maybe I need to hear it now.'

'Hey!'

'What?'

'You've done a good job.'

Ben pulled a face at Kip. 'But seriously, though, why doesn't he talk to me?'

'I told you, it's his English.'

Ben looked over at his grandfather, taking the cows down to the water to drink.

'It's not *that* bad. I'm sure he could say "well done".'

'Dude! Do you know how many times he's said that to *me*?'

Ben looked away.

'Once, bro. Once!'

'Well, that's once more than me.'

'But I've known him my whole life. And have you not noticed how little he speaks to me?'

'What are you talking about? He's always chatting to you.'

'Only to give instructions, or to use me to translate. Maybe I'm the one who should be all upset!' Kip fell to his knees in mock devastation. 'I just feel so used!'

'That's ridiculous!'

'Exactly! Just listen to yourself. Anyway, what's stopping *you* talking to *him*? I don't see you making a big effort to get to know your grandfather.'

Ben shifted his weight from one foot to the other. What would he say to Koipapi, given the opportunity? He was longing to ask him about the blood phobia, but where would he begin?

'Look, bro, don't ruin the moment, you've just done an amazing thing. If Grandpapi wasn't happy, he'd have made you do it again. Which reminds me . . .'

'What?'

'Will you do it again?'

'Why?'

'I want to see how you did it.'

And despite the fact that Ben had absolutely no idea how he had managed such a feat, Kip persuaded him to throw the spear again and again so that he could scrutinize his style. He had hoped to copy it, but eventually conceded that Ben had his father's 'gift'. And this, in Kip's mind, was something that could not be taught.

Later that night, Ben watched his grandfather preparing their evening meal, and the more he waited, the more nervous he became. Several times, he almost gathered the guts to approach him but then his mouth dried up and his legs went all wobbly so he decided to stay where he was.

'What are you doing?' asked Kip, making Ben jump.

'I don't know,' replied Ben, shrugging in embarrassment. 'What should I say?'

'Ask him something.'

'Like what?'

'You want to know about your fear, don't you? Like how to really beat it.'

'Can't you ask him for me?'

'Don't be stupid! Anyway, look, he's calling us over for supper. It's now or never.'

As the boys approached the fire, Koipapi handed them some bowls of soup. Ben took what he was given, but then stood there, frozen like a mime artist, until a glare from his cousin helped him snap out of it.

'Excuse me,' Ben stuttered, too quietly, in the direction of his grandfather, who turned and walked away. His heart sank.

'Try again,' urged Kip, as their grandfather returned with some dried meat, placing it on a rock by the fire.

If he had done it once, he could do it again.

'Grandpapi,' he said, with conviction. But even though he had spoken more loudly, his timing was off. He had blurted it out just as his grandfather was lowering himself down on to his haunches, with a loud grunt that perfectly masked Ben's voice.

He glanced at his cousin. Kip was obviously trying to hide a smirk behind his hand, which fuelled Ben's determination yet further.

'Koipapi!' he bellowed, and his grandfather shot to his feet like he'd just been bitten by a snake. Ben wanted to throw himself on the fire with embarrassment, but at least he had his grandfather's attention now, and it was probably marginally less awkward to plough on than stay silent.

'What do you mean when you say I have only faced my fear, not beaten it?'

Koipapi turned to Kip, presumably for clarification, and they exchanged words back and forth in Maa. Then, just as Ben was wondering whether they might have forgotten about his question and were now discussing the weather, Kip spoke.

'He says you've only looked your fear in the eye. You haven't yet kicked it in the balls.' Kip coughed into his hand, but Ben could see he was actually laughing. It wasn't helping.

'How will I know when I have, er, moved on from looking it in the eye?' asked Ben, undeterred.

This time, they spent even longer discussing his question until at last, Kip turned to him with a straight face. 'Grandpapi says, "You'll know!"'

When they'd finished their food and night had fallen, Koipapi went to sleep quickly as usual, but Kip and Ben stayed up for a while, staring into the fire and talking about the day.

'Can you believe you threw a spear all that way?' asked Kip.

'Not really,' said Ben, grinning. 'I keep forgetting, but it feels really good when I remember again.'

'You glad you talked to Grandpapi too?'

'Urgh!' Ben buried his head in his hands at the memory.

'Ah, come on, at least you have your answer now.'

'Kind of.'

'Why only kind of?'

'I still don't know whether I passed or not.'

Kip buried his forehead in the palm of his hand.

'Kip.'

'What?'

'I just—'

'What?'

'How did you get your "well done" from Koipapi?'

The cloud that Ben had noticed once before began to shadow Kip's face again. It was just perceptible in the darkness.

'You remember what I told you about the poachers threatening to kill me?'

'Yeah?'

'Well, when they let go of me, I got up off the ground, counted all the animals as usual and then locked them up for the night. Grandpapi put his hand on my shoulder and said, "*Ai Sidai*".'

'Well done?'

Kip nodded, and they both gazed into the fire.

'Ben,' said Kip after a while, 'you can't rely on someone else to tell you when you've done a good job. I think you're just going to have to trust you're on the right track.'

'But I thought the whole point was that I had to pass the tests. How will I know if I've passed them, if no one tells me?'

'I didn't hear anybody say you had to pass the tests.'

'What do you mean?'

'It's the challenges themselves that make you strong, not passing them.'

'Oh!'

'*Ngai!* I think I just saw a tiny light come on in your eyes. Well, that's enough thinking for one night, we don't want to tire you out!' Kip opened up his *shuka* and wiggled his eyebrows suggestively at Ben.

'No spooning!' Ben said, and threw a stick at his cousin, who mimed being mortally wounded.

Then Ben lay down, turning his back to the fire to keep it warm for as long as possible. And when he finally drifted off, he dreamt that his father had seen him throw the spear as far as the fourth tree.

CHAPTER 23

~~~~~~~~~~~~~~~~

Every centimetre of Ben's body was aching. He was aware of muscles he never even knew he had, mainly because they hurt so much.

His back was stiff from sleeping on the ground, and his raging hunger did nothing to help his mood. Milk for lunch and meat for dinner was all very well, but what about breakfast? Had they not brought any eggs? For the first time in his life, Ben had dreamt of mashed potato and broccoli. Broccoli!

But there was nothing he could do about that now, and he tried to put it out of his mind as he and Kip walked to their next task. Challenge number five was to bring back the tail hair of a wild animal. The type of animal, Koipapi had said, was not important.

'A cheetah would be cool,' mused Kip. 'They're pretty safe, but we'll never catch one.'

'How about a giraffe?' Ben did his best impression of a giraffe by walking and talking in slow motion.

'Good idea, but one kick from those bad boys – even a baby – and it's game over.'

'What about a lion?'

'Are you kidding?'

'Yes.'

'Thank you, that's very helpful.'

Ben grinned.

'We might be able to sneak up on a rhino,' said Kip. 'But we're in trouble if it hears us coming.'

'Do you have mice here?'

'Bro, there has to be some element of danger.'

'Rats, then? You said you have those.'

'I think it's going to be a warthog,' said Kip, ignoring his cousin. 'Those tusks are serious weapons, man. But its size – we can deal with that.'

The quest for a warthog took the boys along the riverbank for several miles further into the wilderness, and then up and out to the tree line on the edge of the savannah. Immediately the animals came into view. Lots of them.

'I had no idea there would be so many,' whispered Ben. 'It's like a pig farm. Can't we just go and grab one?'

'No way, bro! They will either attack or run away, and we don't want either.'

'What's the plan then?'

'Let's watch the pattern. That's what lions do.'

'The pattern?'

'Yup. They're creatures of habit. If we watch for long enough, we'll see our moment.'

Ben wasn't convinced, but he didn't have anything better to offer, so he supposed it was worth a try. And sure enough, after about an hour, it became clear that Kip was right.

First, the hogs would come out of their hole with their babies and snuffle around for food, and then the moment something spooked them, they would all dive back in, hoglets first.

After about five minutes, the parent pig would have a little look outside, and if the coast was clear, it would come all the way out and stand in front of the hole. Then when it seemed satisfied that everything appeared to be safe enough, all its hoglets would come running out and the whole process started all over again.

'Right!' said Kip. 'When they all go inside – that's our moment!'

'But how will we get a tail hair if all the hogs are inside?'

'Good point, bro. We wait until Mama Hog comes out and then we grab her.'

'Which bit of her?'

Kip laughed. 'You go for the tusks and I'll try and pull out the tail hairs.'

'Wait! I thought you said the tusks are serious weapons . . .'

'They are, but the other end's pretty dangerous too. Just hold on as tight as you can, then when I shout "now" just let go and run away.'

'You done this before?'

'Never!'

'Great!'

'One last thing, though . . .'

Ben rolled his eyes to heaven. Kip whacked him on the arm.

'The den is a bit exposed, we need to take some cover with us.'

They each cut down a small bush to hide behind,

and waited until something scared the hogs and forced them underground. Then they ran. They dashed across the open grassland to the hog's hideout and crashed down into the grass just behind it, covering themselves with their foliage.

The sprint only took about thirty seconds, so they had plenty of time to regain their breath before the warthog's nose reappeared. It sniffed around, then went back in again.

'It must have smelt us,' whispered Kip.

Ben had stopped using sun cream long ago, and was so dirty it felt like he was wearing a second skin, but perhaps he was still too human-smelling.

Then suddenly, before he could work out what to do about it, the warthog shot out of the hole and stood right in front of him.

'Go!' shouted Kip, and they both threw off their bushes, which confused the hog for a split second, long enough for them to jump on her.

Ben grabbed the tusks as tightly as he could. The animal was only about the size of a bulldog, but it was probably just as ferocious, and much stronger than he ever could have imagined. It thrashed backwards and forwards, from side to side, squealing and grunting.

Ben hoped Kip was doing what he should be doing – he was certainly making some very strange noises. Perhaps he was trying to confuse it by pretending to be a warthog, thought Ben.

Then, just as he was beginning to lose his grip, Kip shouted 'Now!' and they ran as fast as possible, back to their lookout on the edge of the trees.

Panting for breath, they turned back to see that the warthog had given up chase and was guarding its hole, staring at the boys, confused and affronted by the outrage that had just taken place.

'What's that?' asked Ben, peering at what looked like mud all over Kip's face.

'Poo,' he replied, trying to wipe it off.

'No!'

'Yup!'

'The pig dumped on your face?'

'Yes, bro,' said Kip resignedly. 'I'd have probably done the same under the circumstances.'

Ben couldn't help but laugh between gasps for breath.

'Oh, go ahead and kick a man when he's down,' said Kip.

Ben looked at his semi-serious but very dirty face. His cousin had a funny face at the best of times, and now there was even poo in his hair and eyebrows. It was impossible not to laugh. And eventually Kip gave in too and they found themselves holding on to each other for support.

It was the kind of laughter that seemed to come from their toes and take over their whole bodies, but by the time it came out of their mouths, it was just squeaks and coughs. Then finally, they collapsed on to the grass, utterly weak but totally triumphant.

CHAPTER 24

▰▰▰▰▰▰▰▰▰▰▰

They stashed the victory hairs in Ben's trainer. Kip had wanted to put them under his toga, but Ben just couldn't see how he would ever find them again. Kip refused to tell him the secret of where he hid everything, so the shoe was settled upon. Then they decided to take a different route back to camp, sticking to the edge of the trees for a while rather than going straight down to the river.

They had been walking for about fifteen minutes when some movement in the bushes stopped them in their tracks.

'What is it?' whispered Ben, alarmed by the look on Kip's face. Kip said nothing.

They both stood, stock still, waiting for the next sign of movement. Then suddenly there came a thin trumpeting sound, and shortly afterwards, a very small elephant, no bigger than a Shetland pony, came crashing through the bushes.

The tiny giant flapped its Dumbo-like ears and made several mock charges towards them. The sound that came from its trunk was no more powerful than a musical toy from a Christmas cracker, and it made Ben want to laugh rather than run away. But Kip put a warning hand across his chest.

'Just wait, bro,' he said. 'If the mother is close by, we are in big-time danger right now.'

They stood frozen to the spot for a few minutes whilst the little elephant disappeared into the bushes and re-emerged repeatedly, attempting to charge them each time.

'It's like he's protecting something,' said Kip quietly.

Then there was the sound of much louder trumpeting from further away, and a large herd of elephants emerged from the edge of the trees a long way ahead of them.

'His mum must be one of those, then,' said Ben, gesturing towards the herd.

'Yeah, but why is he not joining them?'

As the baby elephant disappeared back into the bushes again, Kip pulled at Ben's arm. 'Let's follow it and see if we can get a better look.'

So, they picked their way carefully and quietly through the undergrowth until they came to the other side of the bush.

The little elephant was there before them, nudging at a huge grey mass on the ground, determined to make it move somehow. Now and again the baby would stop and tenderly touch the adult elephant's face with its infant trunk, desperately searching for signs of life. But Ben and Kip had understood instantly what the baby could not.

There were two large, gaping wounds on either side of its mother's head, in the places where her tusks and most of her face should have been. Her side had also been opened up with what Ben thought must be shots from a rifle, and the blood that had recently poured from these wounds was now a dark, matt burgundy.

Ben groaned. He had not been ready for such a sight, nor the tidal wave of crashing despair that followed. Everything about it was so shocking and wrong, like he'd walked into a nightmare without realizing he'd even fallen asleep.

He glanced at Kip, whose hands were covering his mouth as if stifling a scream, then looked back at the horror. His head was swimming, but he knew he was too angry to pass out.

The baby elephant caught sight of the boys and attempted to charge them again, bravely defending its dead mother. Kip waved his arms at it and growled. 'He thinks we're the poachers,' he said, his voice cracking. 'But he has to join the herd or he'll die without his mother. Quick, Ben! Help me!'

Together they ushered the little elephant into the open whilst trying to stay hidden from the herd themselves. Eventually, after many failed attempts, the baby gave in and followed the call of the others in the distance. The boys watched with heavy hearts as the elephants disappeared over the horizon together.

'Would they not have come back for him?' asked Ben, when he was able to speak.

'Maybe. But they were probably too scared.'

'I can't imagine elephants being scared.'

They turned back to the mother, lying dead on the ground.

'You ever seen anything like that before?' asked Ben.

'No,' said Kip, quietly. 'Never.'

The walk back to camp was mostly spent in silence. By the time they arrived, the horror of what they had seen had caught up with them and they could not have spoken even if they had wanted to.

Ben quietly produced the hog's tail hairs from his shoe and held them out in his open hand to allow Koipapi to check them.

'Warthog?' Koipapi asked, examining them closely.

Ben nodded, afraid that if he tried to speak, he might cry. But he needn't have bothered to hide his feelings, because Koipapi stopped peering at the tail hairs and looked up – straight into his eyes.

Ben tried to turn away but his grandfather's gaze stayed on him, burning inwards, searching not just his face but his soul.

Then he looked across at Kip, as if to verify his findings, and just as Ben felt he couldn't bear the scrutiny any longer, their grandfather spoke.

'Sorry, my boys,' he said, as though having looked deep inside them, he had seen things exactly as they were.

They sat round the fire at dusk, picking at their dried meat and soup supper, and Ben checked his phone again for the twentieth time that hour.

'She'll be fine, bro,' said Kip. 'They got their ivory.'

'How could anyone do that?'

'It's worth a lot of money.'

'To who?'

'The Chinese mostly. They turn it into jewellery and stuff.'

Ben shook his head in disbelief.

'Yup!' said Kip. 'Though most of them don't know you have to kill the elephant to get it. They think tusks fall out like milk teeth.'

'If only!' Ben sighed, then jumped as his phone beeped. He quickly opened his messages. 'It's from Mum.'

'What does it say?'

'*Poachers got an elephant* – that must be the one we saw today!' said Ben, before continuing with the message, '*but the rangers captured the stolen ivory and arrested three of the poachers. We got everything on camera.*'

'Yes!' Kip offered Ben a high five, which he returned half-heartedly. 'What's up, bro?'

'They're going to be really angry now . . .'

'Don't worry, bro. It's all part of the plan.'

'What *is* the plan?'

'Well,' Kip said, leaning forward and looking like himself again, 'First, they wind up Shetani by intercepting his kills, capturing the ivory and arresting weaker members of his gang. But most importantly, they make it really obvious that they're getting loads of incriminating footage. Bit like poking a stick in a beehive, stealing the honey and taking pictures.'

Ben snorted a laugh, and some soup sprayed on to Kip's face.

'Bro!'

'Sorry.'

'Then just when Shetani's about ready to kill me, my dad's going to give them a fake tip-off that everyone is out for the day, and all the footage is left unguarded. They'll go to the lodge, thinking they're going to seize everything, but what they don't know, is that the rangers will be there, ready to arrest them. And our lot are going to hide, but leave the cameras running so everything's caught on film.'

'Wow!' said Ben.

'Yes, bro! That's my dad!' Kip did a mini version of his victory dance, but from a sitting position on his log.

'Kip?'

'Whassup?'

'Aren't you scared?'

Kip looked away. 'What do you mean?'

'Well, are you sure *you're* safe out here in the bush? That elephant was only a few miles away; the poachers must have been pretty close to us last night.'

'Yeah, but the rangers just arrested three of them, didn't they? The others'll want to lie low for a few days. Like I said – all part of the plan!'

'You're brave, you know. I'm bricking it and they don't even know I'm here.'

'Aw, shucks, bro!' said Kip. He lifted a corner of his *shuka*. 'You want a hug?'

'No!' said Ben.

CHAPTER 25

B en lay alongside his cousin in the grass. The sun beating down on his head was unbearably hot, but inside he just felt cold and empty.

After seeing the elephant yesterday, it was like a switch had flipped inside him. That night he had lain awake for a long time, thinking about the baby separated from its mother, and it made him think of his own mum and the danger she was in. Senteu's plan sounded amazing, but what if the poachers just took a shortcut and went straight for her instead?

In the morning, he had woken early and let himself into the *boma*. The animals were comfortingly just the same as normal, and he had walked amongst them, stopping now and then to stroke them or lean on them, absorbing their warmth. He found the young calf he had delivered, nuzzling its mother whilst her breath curled upwards into the crisp morning air.

But there was no getting away from today's task. And Kip had said it would be the most difficult one yet – to hunt and kill a wild animal for their food.

'First, you must speak to the animals,' Kip explained, as they watched the herd of gazelle. 'And ask who would like to give their life for us today. Then, when they show themselves, you strike.'

'Wait a minute,' said Ben, nervously grasping the rock Kip had given him. 'What do you mean, speak to the animals?'

'You know – with your mind.'

Ben looked like he'd just been given an impossible riddle to solve.

'OK, I guess you *don't* know,' said Kip. 'Well, just think about asking the question, but sort of send it to the animal with your mind.'

A gentle breeze stirred the long grass in front of them, carrying with it the mournful cry of a lapwing.

'So, have you asked?' said Kip.

Ben nodded.

'Well, get ready, bro. The first time is always the hardest.'

At last, one of the gazelle raised its head above the grass.

'There it is!' exclaimed Kip, and in one slick movement, he leapt up and threw the rock he'd been clutching.

It just missed the animal, but Ben's was right behind it. The stone had left his hand, before he'd even realized he was on his feet. Then it flew through the air with missile speed and met with its target perfectly.

'Shot, bro!' gasped Kip.

There was no visible blood on the gazelle, but it was obvious that some damage had been done when it began to move strangely.

'This'll be hard to watch,' warned Kip.

The wounded animal did not go down immediately, but ran erratically in various directions. Now and again it would shake its head, fall to its knees and then get up again.

Ben could feel Kip watching him, expecting him to look away, and though he held his gaze on the gazelle, he wished, more than anything, that he could reverse what had just happened, drop the rock he had been holding only seconds ago, and walk away.

After about a minute, the gazelle went down and stayed there and Kip set out towards it, a new rock in his hand.

'Wait!' Ben stuttered. 'I–I'm not sure it's dead yet.' But he followed his cousin nevertheless, hanging back slightly, barely able to look.

As they neared the animal, Ben could see it was twitching slightly, eyes wide open with a trickle of blood coming from its nose. Kip stood over it and paused for a second to set his sights, then he hit it twice on the head with the rock.

'Now it is,' said Kip.

When the boys returned to camp with the gazelle, Koipapi sent them off to tend the cattle whilst he got to work turning the animal into food. Ben watched from a distance as their grandfather skinned and disembowelled the beast, then pushed a spit through its entire length. He suspended the carcass over the glowing embers of a second fireplace he had constructed between two trees, using poles and ropes he had presumably brought for the purpose. Then he sat on a log nearby, occasionally turning the gazelle to ensure it was evenly cooked, but it would be a long time before the meat was ready.

The boys spent the hours grazing and watering the cattle, and Ben was grateful that Kip seemed to share his need for silence. His brain seemed to be churning so loudly, though, he wondered if Kip could actually hear it. He was so angry with the poachers for what they had done to the elephant, but how was *he* any better? Would his dad have been proud of him for killing a gazelle? What would his mum think? He wondered whether she and Uncle Senteu had set the trap yet and felt a fresh wave of worry.

Finally, when it was almost time to eat, Koipapi called the boys and they secured the cattle in the pen before sitting down by the fire.

Ben had had no appetite for anything except water all day, and he felt no differently now. He was expecting to be handed some meat and was trying to think of a polite way of declining, when Koipapi and Kip sat down beside him and gazed into the fire, feeding the flames with dry kindling that crackled and spat.

Much to Ben's surprise, no one offered him anything, and just as he was thinking he might lie down and cover himself with his *shuka* to escape the awkwardness, his cousin spoke.

'Our grandfather has something to say,' said Kip. 'He wants to tell you himself, but he says that it's important that you really know his mind and so he has asked me to translate. Is that OK?'

Ben nodded, silenced by the sudden air of formality between them.

Koipapi began to speak, and even though Ben didn't understand the language, his grandfather's tone seemed to be filled with a new kind of tenderness that immediately captured his attention.

'Grandpapi says,' began Kip, 'that he understands why the death of the elephant made you angry and sad.' He paused for a moment, listening to his grandfather's words before continuing. 'But he wants you to know that it's OK to feel this way. He feels it too.'

Ben's heart was racing – he wasn't aware that his grandfather had noticed anything about him at all.

Kip went on, 'He also knows that it hurt you to kill the gazelle today, and that you're trying to hide your pain.' Kip stopped to listen to Koipapi, and Ben hoped that neither of them would see his face flushing with embarrassment. He could feel a lump rising in his throat now too.

His cousin continued. 'He says, you are part of the land and the animals. It is normal to feel their pain. The elephant's life was taken for nothing, it was a waste, but the gazelle is different. Grandpapi says that whenever you feel bad about what you did, you must remember that you asked for her permission, and then thank the animal for her sacrifice. Her flesh will feed your body and make you strong. Her spirit will enable you to jump high like a true warrior.'

Ben could feel a tidal wave of pressure building up behind his eyes, and he wished it would turn back. But Kip and his grandfather carried on.

'Grandpapi says, you have shown him that you are a true Maasai even before you have met the last challenge.'

Koipapi took Ben's hand and looked straight into his eyes with a smile. '*Ai sidai!*' he said.

And that was it. Hot tears poured down Ben's face, and his body convulsed as pent-up sobs of emotion rushed to the surface.

Koipapi pulled him into his chest and held him there as he wept. Then, just as Ben was thinking he should stop crying and behave like a man, he felt a drop of water fall on to his head from above and looked up to see that his grandfather was also wiping tears from his own cheeks.

Ben turned away to save his grandfather's embarrassment, but the old man simply held him tighter, rocking him gently back and forth until all their tears were spent.

It could have been an hour that they stayed that way or perhaps just five minutes, but once Ben had given in to his tears, it was as though he had conceded the fight on all fronts, and he could quite easily have fallen asleep right where he was. Out of nowhere, Kip produced a bowl of hot soup and held it out to Ben.

'Take it,' said Koipapi. 'You feel better.'

His grandfather was right and as he drank the hot, soothing liquid, he could feel not only his strength beginning to return, but also his hunger. Somehow this was understood and Ben was passed pieces of fresh, juicy meat that he devoured ravenously.

Even though the gazelle was truly delicious, now and again a picture of the animal in distress would enter his mind. And he would have to pause and give thanks, as his grandfather had suggested, so that he could go on eating. But there was something about the hot food that gave him a feeling of deep satisfaction, and very soon he was ready for sleep.

As usual it was Koipapi who pulled his *shuka* over his head first. The boys did their utmost to stay awake and speculate on the seventh and final challenge, but it was only a matter of minutes before their tiredness became too much for them. Ben kept telling himself to turn his back to the fire and avoid a sore back, but in the end, he fell asleep before he could summon the energy to move.

It was impossible to know how long they had been sleeping when Ben heard Koipapi shuffle to his feet, but it couldn't have been many hours that had passed because the fire was still crackling. He assumed his grandfather was fetching more wood but then, much to his surprise, the old man lay down on the ground directly behind him.

Ben opened his eyes a crack – Kip was still fast asleep across from them – why had Grandpapi moved? Perhaps he was uncomfortable. Ben could understand that, it usually took him ages to find a good spot, without too many stones or twigs.

He was just about to roll over and give up his place to his grandfather when a *shuka* was draped over him, immediately cutting off the biting draught, and enveloping him in the heat of his grandfather's body as it curled around his own.

Ben didn't know whether he should turn around and say, 'thank you', but it was as though he'd been given a general anaesthetic suddenly and was too sleepy to speak. And finally, with his back properly warm for the first time in nearly a week, he fell fast asleep.

CHAPTER 26

‘Do you feel more black or white?’ asked Kip, as they packed up their camp for the last time.

‘That’s a funny question,’ said Ben. ‘Why do you ask?’

‘Well, I was just thinking you’re a bit like Obama, with your Kenyan dad and your white mum.’

‘I suppose.’

‘White people call him black, but some black people think he’s too white. I always wanted to ask him how *he* feels. Now I can ask you.’

‘You’re asking me how Barack Obama feels?’ said Ben.

‘No, *you*! Do you think of yourself as black or white?’

'I dunno,' replied Ben. 'It depends.'

'But did you ever want to be more of one thing than the other?'

'Not really. But then I never had the full picture, till I met you lot.'

Kip crossed his eyes and Ben sniggered.

'I once saw this Nigerian woman on the news,' said Kip. 'She said she never heard herself described as black until she went to college in America.'

'Huh! In my school, they call white people "peach" now.'

'What do they call you?'

'Ben.'

Kip threw his *shuka* at him.

'Where do you watch the news?' asked Ben, throwing back the blanket.

'Online, dummy!'

'Yeah, but where?'

'Oh, at the camp. I watch the news, documentaries, stuff like that. They have loads of magazines too.'

'What, like *Vogue*?'

Kip threatened to throw his *shuka* back.

'No, they have *Time*, *The Week*, *The Economist*. Trevor lets me read them all. Though it's all going to come to an end if the poachers keep killing our elephants. No elephants, no tourists. No tourists, no camp.'

'That's what Trevor said.'

'He's right! I love that place. I met Bill Gates there once, and Larry Page. Loads of famous people stay there.'

'Who's Larry Page?'

'One of the founders of Google,' said Kip. 'Where have you been all your life?'

'I met him once, you know,' said Ben.

'Larry Page?'

'Barack Obama.'

'No way!'

'Yeah, my mum interviewed him for a documentary.'

'What was he like?'

'Really cool! He told me to follow my dreams.'

'What are your dreams?'

Ben looked away.

'Come on! Tell me!'

'I want to be a doctor,' said Ben, relieved that it didn't sound as silly as he thought it would.

'That's cool, man! But if it doesn't work out, you could always be President of the United States.'

'I'd have to settle for Prime Minister of England.'

'Or Kenya? You can be President—'

'And you can be Prime Minister—'

'Yes, bro. Then we could lock up all the poachers.'

'And the elephants would be OK.'

'And the tourists would come back . . .'

Ben hoisted the panniers on to the carrier donkey. 'Kip, what happens if they *don't* come back? How will you survive?'

'We'd live off the cows, I guess, until you came back for them . . .' Kip kicked at a dry divot of earth. 'We could always come and live with you in London.'

'We'd need a bigger flat.'

'Dude, have you seen the size of *our* house?'

'Yeah, but where would we put the cows?'

'Good point. And talking of the cows, let's check we've got everybody.'

Koipapi and the boys counted all the livestock and did a thorough check of the camp to ensure nothing was left behind. Then they took it in turns to pee on the fire and thanked Ngai for their safety.

'Kip!' said Ben, just as they were about to set off.

'Yes, cuz?'

'I've been thinking.'

'Uh-oh!'

'Would it help if I gave you my cows?' Ben blurted it out, then they both looked at each other, holding their breath.

'Are you serious, bro?' said Kip eventually.

'Absolutely! But do you think the firstborn son of the firstborn son is allowed to give his cattle to the firstborn son of the second-born son?'

Kip stroked an imaginary beard. 'Maybe if the first-born son of the firstborn son asked his grandfather for permission to give his cows to the second-born son, then the second-born son could decide whether to give them to *his* firstborn son.' Kip held his hand up for a high five.

'Nice!' said Ben, giving his palm a resounding slap.

'Seriously, though, Ben, would you really do that for us?'

'Of course! They're your cows really. You love them and they love you.'

'Bro!'

'I've seen the way they look at you.'

'Who, *me*?' Kip said, batting his eyelids.

*

The rest of the morning was spent herding the cows back along the river, so they could enjoy the green grass for a few more hours before heading home to the dryness of the village. It was like a lesson in Maasai medicine, with Kip pointing out all the different plants and what they could be used for. Ben's favourite was the Toothbrush Bush. Kip showed him how to cut off a twig and use it to clean his teeth, chewing and fraying out the end to make it like a brush and using the other, sharper side like a tooth pick. Having gone without brushing for almost five whole days, it was every bit as good as an actual toothbrush and toothpaste.

Sometime in the late afternoon, they stopped to eat, and though the gazelle had tasted better the night before, there was much satisfaction in knowing it was food they'd worked for. After they had eaten, they rested for a few moments as usual. Ben lay in the grass and thought about how much better he felt now than he had a week ago. Perhaps it was because he'd had a good night's sleep at last. He didn't have the guts to tell Kip that he'd let Koipapi spoon with him – he knew he'd say, 'I told you so.' But he felt so much stronger now, and with only one challenge left to complete, the end was finally in sight.

He'd only been in Kenya just over a week but already home felt very far away. The endless sky was something he would certainly miss in Hackney, he thought, gazing upwards. Then, as if the weather was trying to make it easier on him, a pod of clouds scudded into view.

'Huh!'

'What?' asked Kip, casually checking his phone.

'Those are the first clouds I've seen since I got here.'

'Well, look over there if you want to see clouds.'

Ben looked in the direction his cousin was pointing. The sky was like an aubergine-coloured bruise that seemed to be spreading towards them. There wasn't a chink of blue to be seen anywhere.

'Wow!' said Ben. 'Shouldn't we get going?'

'Oh!' Kip sat up suddenly.

'What's wrong?'

'I just got a text from my dad.'

'What does it say?'

'He's telling us not to go to the lodge tomorrow when we get back.'

'Why?'

'They've had to put back the set-up until tomorrow afternoon because the rangers are busy with the poachers they arrested.'

'That gives me the creeps!'

'Me too! I thought they were going to do "Operation Poacher Grab" yesterday, or today at the latest. You heard from your mum?'

'Don't think so.' Ben glanced at his phone, feeling guilty suddenly for not having checked it all day. 'Oh, wait! There's a message here!' He clicked the little envelope icon. '*Hi, my love. Can't wait to see you tomorrow. Do NOT come to the lodge, we'll come to you. We'll be there by 4 p.m. Pls let me know you've got this. Love you. Mum xx*' Ben stared at Kip.

'Well, what are you waiting for?' urged Kip.

'Oh, right, yeah.' Ben's heart was pounding and his fingers felt completely useless, but he managed to fire off a quick message all the same: *Hi mum, got ya msg. will w8 for U. Gd luk. luv u 2*

'Kipat!' said Koipapi suddenly, making the boys jump. Kip scrambled to his feet to listen to his grandfather's instructions for the final challenge.

'OK,' announced Kip, when Koipapi had finished speaking. 'This is it! The BIG ONE!'

Ben nodded in anticipation.

'Challenge seven,' said Kip, 'is to take the cows home.'

The boys stared at each other.

'Is that it?' asked Ben.

'I think so,' said Kip. 'Koipapi says we have the choice of going now or waiting for morning. But if we go now, most of our journey will be in darkness.'

'Is that a problem?'

'I don't think so. I can find my way home with my eyes shut . . .'

So why did it all feel so strange? wondered Ben. He hadn't expected the last challenge to be so . . . unchallenging. And Kip looked no less confused than Ben felt. The boys continued to stare at each other, as if any second now, one or the other might come up with an explanation. Then finally Koipapi spoke directly to Ben, dramatically bringing home the overall sense of weirdness. 'Benedict!' he said. 'Son of my son, when you feel fear, call on your father. Ngai be with you!'

And off he walked, out of the tree line, across the savannah and into the falling darkness.

CHAPTER 27

'**R**ight!' said Ben. 'Shall we get it over and done with, then? If we go now, at least we can follow Grandpapi.'

'Er, I like your thinking, but that won't work, because he's gone the wrong way.'

'What? Well, shouldn't we go after him then – make sure he's OK?'

'No, he's done it deliberately – to throw us off,' said Kip.

'Are you sure? It looks like the right way to me.'

'Of course I'm sure. The escarpment is over there,' he said, waving his arm at a forty-five degree angle away from the route their grandfather had taken.

As they gazed into the distance, the sky seemed to change before their eyes. A full moon was beginning to fill the plain with an eerie blue light. But the clouds that passed across it became steadily more frequent, until eventually it was completely obscured and they could see their grandfather no longer.

'I think we should get going,' said Kip. 'Don't you?' Ben nodded and they began gathering up their few belongings and loading them on to the donkey. Then, just as they finished securing the last item, Ben noticed a drop of water on his face.

'Did you feel that?' he said.

'What?'

'Rain, I think,' said Ben.

'Oh, no!' said Kip. 'That's all we need. Well, let's gather the herd and get out of here.'

Ben turned around to call the cows, only to find that a thick mist had crept up behind them and the rain was now steadily increasing. He whipped back to check the donkey was still there, but discovered the donkey was all he could see. The mist had covered everything more efficiently than a smoke machine.

'OK, don't panic,' said Kip, sounding panicked. 'The cows won't go anywhere in this. We'll just have to sit it out.'

'Should we light a fire?'

'Not much point, really – it'll probably pass soon.'

But it didn't.

They hunkered down under a tree, and though it gave them some shelter, they still managed to become wet through in no time.

'Do you think Grandpapi knew this was going to happen?' asked Ben, hunched against the cold.

''Course he did. It would have been too easy otherwise.'

Ben wondered if predators came out in the rain, then realized that the cows had no pen to protect them. He turned to Kip to ask what they should do about it, only to find that his eyes were closed.

'Kip,' he whispered.

Nothing. *Great*, thought Ben. *Now what do I do?*

He considered waking him, but then decided the best thing would be to keep guard for an hour or so. Sleeping was off the cards anyway with this much adrenaline pumping round his body.

Though the rain on the tree canopy was loud, Koipapi's words were still ringing in his head: *when you feel fear, call on your father.* And he had looked at

Ben so intensely – perhaps he really meant it.

The sad thing was, Ben wished he *could* call on his father.

He thought back over all the challenges he had completed over the last week. Kip had also suggested he talk to his dad, but he had never actually done it because it seemed too crazy. But as he sat there, propped up against the tree in the pouring rain, it suddenly occurred to him that each time he had felt incapable of the task ahead, he had thought of his father in *some* way or another, and then there was always a kind of strength – a fleeting sense of something greater than him – helping him. He certainly had no idea how he had done it all on his own.

He glanced at his cousin sleeping next to him, his *shuka* wrapped around his ears against the rain and the cold. *It can't be any weirder than speaking to an animal with your mind*, he thought. *What do I have to lose?*

'OK, Dad,' whispered Ben. 'If it's at all possible, I could really use some warrior help right now.'

He had no memory of falling asleep, but when he woke, the mist had gone and everything was bathed in a ghostly blue light from the full moon again. All around them lay the familiar sight of brown cow-shaped mounds. Ben breathed a sigh of relief, but decided to count them anyway, just to be sure.

One donkey, one goat, one calf and thirty-one cows. Thirty-one? How had they gained a cow? Resolving that he must have miscounted, he was just about to begin again when one of the brown shapes shook itself and Ben stopped breathing.

There, lying in the grass amidst the sleeping cows, was the unmistakable silhouette of a huge male lion.

As slowly as he could, Ben reached for Kip's arm, and when an earnest squeeze produced no response, he dug his nails into the flesh.

'*Ngai!*' yelped Kip. 'What are you—'

Ben squeezed again and nodded in the direction of the predator.

'What the . . .' Kip's voice trailed off.

'Why are the cows not freaking out?' whispered Ben.

'I have no idea,' said Kip, speaking each word very slowly as though his brain was grinding to a halt.

The lion shook its mane again and Kip grabbed Ben's hand. Then the great cat stood up, turned its back and started moving away. It walked to the edge of the trees, where it hesitated and looked back over its shoulder at Ben and Kip. Then, as if it was waiting for them, it sat down again.

'Do you think he wants us to follow him?' asked Ben.

'Are you kidding me?' gasped Kip. 'Follow him where?'

'Is he going in the right direction for the village?'

'Er . . . yes.'

'Maybe he wants to take us home.'

'Ben. It's a lion.'

Ben began moving, very slowly, towards the animal.

'*Ngai!* What are you doing?'

The lion got up and started walking away again. Ben stopped, the lion stopped too.

'See!' said Ben over his shoulder. 'He's waiting for us.'

Kip walked up behind Ben. 'OK, bro, I only hope you're right. Because if you're not, I won't be alive to tell everyone this stupid idea was yours.'

Together they nudged the cows awake, anticipating their panic on seeing the lion, but finding only the usual bovine sluggishness. They seemed completely unaware that their ultimate nemesis was sitting right there in front of them. When the lion seemed satisfied that the boys were serious, it got up again and walked off ahead of them. And without any further discussion, everyone seemed to know what to do.

Ben followed at a comfortable distance and behind him Kip herded the cows. Ben had to keep turning around to see if they were still there, because his cousin wasn't giving any of the usual commands. It was as though they were all sleepwalking, drawn by an invisible force.

And so they moved silently onwards – a motley ghost army with the King of Beasts in vanguard position – across the open plain and up the escarpment. Until finally the *manyatta* came into view.

With each passing moment, as they drew closer to the village, Ben felt a bubbling-up of excitement and nerves. It was the kind of incredulous joy that you feel when you know you are right about something really important, but cannot tell anyone.

Then, as day began to break, and they had all but a hundred metres to go, the lion peeled off in a wide arc, then stopped and turned back, as if to ensure the boys might finish their journey safely.

When Koipapi came out to greet them, they watched him with excitement, waiting for the reaction of shock they assumed was inevitable. But he simply smiled and placed his hands across their shoulders, gently encouraging them to go inside. The lion sat at a distance, proudly watching the gathered assembly – even from afar, he exuded a power that made words seem useless.

Reluctantly, the boys turned away from him and moved towards the *manyatta*, looking back over their shoulders with every other step. Koipapi's eyes also remained fixed upon the lion, and when the boys finally stood at the threshold of the *manyatta*, he watched the animal rise to its feet. They gazed at each other – old man and lion – as if some deeper understanding was passing between them. Then finally, Koipapi smiled and whispered a message into the waiting wind.

'Thank you, my son,' he said.

As if satisfied, the lion turned and walked away.

CHAPTER 28

~~~~~~~~~~~~~~~~

The smile on Granny Koko's face was huge. As soon as she saw them, she took the boys by the hand and pulled them into the cosy den of her house, muttering excitedly in Maa. She produced a big bowl of warm milk for them to share, then set to work pulling off their soaking wet trainers. It was much nicer than having a hyena do it, but Ben still felt a bit uncomfortable. He probably hadn't had someone fiddle with his feet since he was a toddler.

'You've done it, bro,' said Kip, as Koko took the shoes outside to dry. 'Can you believe it?'

'Not really!' Ben grinned. It felt like a year rather than a week since he'd last been in this hut, but the sense of achievement was better than he ever could have imagined. And now that the cocooning warmth of Granny Koko's house was beginning to seep into his bones, Ben thought he might just dissolve altogether.

'I don't think I've ever felt this tired,' said Kip.

'Me neither!'

'Sleep . . .' Kip groaned, and crawled on his hands and knees to the little bed behind the curtain then climbed in.

Ben followed like a zombie and was just about to lie down next to Kip, when he caught sight of a small shelf on the wall, above his head. It was littered with different-sized photographs – some framed, some not. As Ben's eye ran along the shelf, he noticed that the pictures all seemed to be of the same child, growing older through the years. He felt a strange sense of familiarity about them and as he looked closer, he realized they were not pictures taken in the Mara, or even Kenya – they were images of London. Then at last his eye fell upon a photo of his own mum standing next to a tiny toddler, who stretched up to hold her hand. It was him. These were all pictures of him.

He turned them over one by one – each had an inscription on the back: *To Koko and Koipapi – Benedict,*

October 23rd – With love, Kate. So she might not have told him about the letters but she had done this. *Every year.* He longed to see her suddenly, but tiredness overwhelmed him and he flopped down next to his cousin. And no sooner had his head touched the scratchy straw mattress than he was fast asleep.

It took Ben a few moments to work out where he was when Kip shook him awake.

'What time is it?' he asked, rubbing his eyes.

'Like, three o'clock or something. Put these on.' Kip was dangling his trainers in his face. Granny Koko had dried them miraculously, but when their smell hit him, Ben wondered if she shouldn't have just burnt them instead.

As he sat up to pull them on, he noticed it wasn't as dead quiet as it had been when they fell asleep. In fact, it sounded like there was a big crowd outside.

'What's that noise?'

'It's party time, bro! Let's go!'

The boys staggered out into the sunlight and Ben almost took two steps backwards. The previously quiet little *manyatta* was thrumming with people, and there were more coming through the gates. The smell of barbecue hit them immediately and Ben's stomach growled in response.

'What's all this about?' asked Ben.

'It's for you, you idiot!' Kip slapped him hard across the back. 'They're giving us a ceremony for returning warriors.'

Then suddenly a rickety old motorbike skidded noisily inside the gates and two elders tipped off it.

'Well, I've never seen that before!' laughed Ben.

'Oh, yeah! That's a Maasai taxi! They've probably come from far.'

They watched as the driver of the bike parked it by the gate and went and helped himself to some barbecue.

'Do all Maasai taxi drivers do that?' asked Ben.

'Like I told you, it's a big party! Come on bro, follow me!'

Kip pulled Ben by the wrist through the crowd to a place in the back corner of the *manyatta*, right up against the fence, where Granny Koko was waiting for them. There were two other women with her, and several little bowls at her feet, filled with different coloured powders and liquids. She stood up when she saw them coming, and the boys came to a standstill in front of her.

With a broad smile, she placed her hands lovingly on their faces. Then, as she turned away to pick up a bowl with a white liquid in it, Kip pulled Ben down to a kneeling position. Koko turned back and poured some of the liquid over Kip's head. He gave a little gasp.

'What's that?' whispered Ben.

'Milk, bro!' Kip was grinning like a child on Christmas morning.

Then Ben watched as their grandmother silently shaved all traces of hair from Kip's already closely-cropped head. When it was Ben's turn, she struck up a gentle, lilting melody that sounded vaguely familiar, and as she stroked his hair in preparation for the milk and the razor, he noticed himself beginning to relax. But this wouldn't be his normal response to someone who was about to shave off his little gold-tipped locks. And then he recognized Koko's tune to be the same as Kip's love song to the cows. He smiled to himself. So it worked on humans too.

When both boys' heads had been shaved, another bowl was passed to their grandmother.

'Red ochre,' whispered Kip.

Koko used her hands to paint their heads with the oily red balm, massaging their skulls until Ben thought he might start drooling, it felt so soothing. But then Kip pulled Ben to his feet and saved him from the embarrassment just in time.

'This is for us to use,' Kip said, dipping his fingers into a wet, chalky paste that filled the last remaining bowl.

First, he traced Ben's hairline with the white paint, and said, 'Heart of lion.' Then he drew a curve on his chin, 'Spirit of gazelle.' Finally, he made three marks, one under each of Ben's eyes, and the third on his forehead. 'Three straight arrows,' he said. 'Your father's father, your father and you.'

Then he took big handfuls of the wet paste and smeared it all over Ben's legs from his ankle to the top of his thigh. And just as Ben thought he must have finished, Kip began dragging his fingernails though the paint, making a repeating pattern of straight and jagged lines. Then at last, he stepped back to admire his handiwork.

'Right!' he said, nodding with satisfaction. 'My turn now,' and he passed the bowl to Ben.

'What do I do?' asked Ben nervously.

'Make me look beautiful, of course!'

Ben dipped his fingers into the paste, but didn't really know what to do next.

'Check out the warriors!' said Kip gesturing to a group of five huge men, covered in painted patterns and dripping with decoration. 'Just go with your imagination, bro!'

Ben started with Kip's legs, using the warriors as a template, but then they moved away and so he had to do his own thing – drawing swirls and squiggles that made Kip laugh. Then gathering confidence from this, Ben moved to his cousin's face.

First, he put a tiny dot of paint on Kip's forehead and said, 'Brain of ant.' Kip pulled his best 'stupid' face in response. Then Ben drew white circles round each of Kip's eyes and said, 'Eyes like a bat.' Kip tried feeling for Ben's face like a blind person. 'And finally,' said Ben, trying not to laugh whilst drawing a line around the entire circle of Kip's face, 'Face like . . .' Kip narrowed his eyes. '. . . A warthog!' shouted Ben and ran away. Kip chased him round a complete circuit of the *manyatta*, grunting like a pig all the way.

When they arrived back at Granny Koko's little

stand, she held up a broken piece of mirror for Kip to see himself.

'Not bad, actually,' he said, gazing at his own reflection.

With tears beginning to run down her cheeks, Granny Koko then turned the mirror in Ben's direction, holding it at just the right angle so he could see all of himself. Ben realized it was about a week since he had last caught sight of his own reflection, and the boy looking back at him now was unrecognizable.

His red toga was just a dirty rag, but somehow it looked better that way. His arms were darker, his legs stronger and the paint on his face and body gave him an air of fierceness.

'What do you think?' asked Kip.

'All right,' said Ben, quietly. He couldn't wait to see the look on his mum's face when she saw him. And suddenly he realized that she still wasn't there.

'Kip!' he gasped. 'What time is it? They must have caught the poachers by now.'

'Good point, bro! Well, they said four p.m., so I'm sure they'll be here any minute.'

Ben gazed over the hedge and up the hill.

'They'll be fine, Ben,' said Kip, pulling him away.

'The rangers are there with some badass rifles. Shetani and his guys? Probably in prison already! Now, let's go and show off!'

CHAPTER 29

The cows had been sent out of the *manyatta* with some young herdsmen to make way for all the visitors. There were no young people chanting and singing this time, no grandmothers ululating; all the noise was that of people talking and laughing, telling stories. In fact, no one seemed that interested in the boys at all, and although this was mildly disappointing, Ben felt relieved not to be stared at.

There were three huge fireplaces that he could see, and each had a metal frame that was heavily laden with sizzling meat. Several animal skins, that looked like they recently belonged to the food now on the barbecue, were hanging on sticks nearby. Then, in the centre, stood a solitary and rather nervous-looking black bullock.

'Is that where the blood will come from?' asked Ben, attempting to sound unconcerned.

'Probably! That's my dad's best young bull,' said Kip, and Ben's skin prickled with excitement and nerves.

Then suddenly Kip grabbed Ben's arm again. 'Look!' he said, pointing at the warriors. 'They're going to jump for you.'

The six formidably tall men had started to sing with deep and serious voices and everyone was gathering around them.

Ben was pulled through the crowd to the front, by various people he didn't know. Then, as if they had been waiting for the guest of honour, the warriors changed their song to a guttural, grunting sound that made the hairs on the back of Ben's neck stand on end.

The powerful rhythm created by the muscular voices grabbed Ben immediately, and began drawing him in. It was pulling on an invisible rope that seemed attached to his gut, and there was no defence against it. It made his skin tingle and stirred something deep inside him, something that wanted to explode outwards.

Ben could sense his thighs tensing, as if gathering

readiness for a huge feat of strength. His hands began to open at his sides, like wings unfurling, ready to lift him up into the air on the bellows rhythm of the warriors' song.

Two of the young men suddenly stepped forward and began to jump on the spot in time to the rise and fall of their peers' voices. Each time they seemed to strain to the furthest extent of their strength, they would give an extra push and go a few centimetres higher.

The others continued to chant and sing, urging them on, and without any signal that Ben could detect, the next two would take a turn.

As he looked around, he noticed that all the faces in the rapt crowd were smiling. It was like everything was right with the world because these men were in their element. And right then Ben understood it. Powerfully, in the very centre of his being, it made sense to him, and he wanted to shout it out loud. Then one of the warriors, sensing Ben's need, invited him to take a turn and he stepped forward as if into a spotlight.

Ready.

He had never felt so ready for anything and as he turned to face the crowd, he knew with absolute certainty that his mum would be there, watching him. This was why she hadn't arrived yet, because the perfect moment for her to see his transformation was just about to take place.

And he jumped. And jumped. Higher and higher, as if the ground was helping him – pushing him further. He held his breath and scanned the crowd, ready to make eye contact at last with his proud, smiling mother. But instead, his eyes were drawn to the now familiar figure of his cousin, who was holding his phone in the air as if to indicate he'd just received a message. And there was no smile of any kind upon his panic-stricken face.

Ben fell down as if punched in the stomach, then quickly scrambled to his feet and pushed through the crowd.

'The rangers didn't make it!' Kip yelled as he drew closer.

'What do you mean?' Ben shouted, straining to hear him above the sounds of the party that just continued around them as if nothing was happening.

'Dad just texted me,' Kip said, holding out his phone with hands that were visibly shaking. 'He's hiding in the storeroom behind the bar with your mum, and they can hear the poachers outside looking for them. We need to call the rangers – NOW!'

'Have you got the number?' Ben gasped.

'Yes, bro!' Kip lifted the phone to his ear and Ben paced back and forth, eyes on the phone, desperate to hear that the rangers were on their way.

'The line's dead . . .' said Kip.

'Phone the police! We have to phone the police!'

'No, bro, I told you, it's not the same here. We can call them, but they'll take half the day to come.'

'I'll phone Mum, then – make sure she's OK.'

'NO! The poachers will hear her phone!'

'Urgh! I can't stand here doing NOTHING!' screamed Ben.

'Let's go then! Maybe we can create a diversion or something. Come on!'

Instinctively, they both ran for the Maasai taxi that was still parked by the gate.

'Do you know how to drive one of these?' shouted Ben.

'Yes, bro!' Kip replied, leaping on the front and starting the engine. He hesitated for only the few seconds it took Ben to jump on behind him, then he twisted the accelerator towards himself and they sped off, out of the gates, leaving a cloud of dust and cow dung behind them.

In actual fact, Kip had only ever ridden a motorbike twice before. But this was, without doubt, the fastest he'd ever done it, and they definitely would have reached the lodge in just a few minutes – if there'd been enough fuel in the tank . . .

The engine spluttered to a standstill halfway up the final hill, but the boys leapt off the bike without hesitation and sprinted onwards as fast as they could.

Gasping for air, lungs and legs burning, they rounded the hill and the camp came into view at last. It took them all of two seconds to register the familiar dirty-grey pickup that was parked outside.

The boys dropped to their stomachs and looked around for cover. Kip pointed to a lone but very thick bush to their right. Trying to remain as low to the ground as possible, they shuffled behind it so they could at least raise their heads slightly without being noticed.

'Can you see anything?' asked Ben, rubbing his elbows as Kip peered through the lower branches.

'Well,' Kip whispered, fighting for breath, 'there's a driver waiting in the pickup, then I think I can see another one of the poachers with a gun, moving around inside . . . it looks like three of our guys, Jez Trevor and Phil, I think, on the floor . . . and there are some lodge staff lying on the ground too, I can just make out their uniforms . . . then there's a pair of red shoes sticking out from behind the bar—'

Kip realized what he'd said just as Ben was scrambling to his feet and making a break for the lodge. But he still managed to tackle Ben to the ground and drag him back behind the bush by his feet.

'Get off!' growled Ben, lashing out at Kip with flailing arms, eventually making contact with his face.

Kip somehow managed to fight his way on top of Ben, eyes and nose stinging from the blows, and pin his arms down by his sides.

'You said he would look after her,' Ben exploded, thrashing from side to side and kicking his legs violently. 'You lied! YOU LIED!'

'Keep your voice down, you idiot!' growled Kip, trying to keep his cousin on the ground. 'My dad is in there too, you know, and if they've found your mum, they've found him as well!'

The boys stared at each other, eyes wide, temples pounding.

'Right!' said Kip, between breaths. 'We need to think.'

Ben pushed him off and rolled over.

'OK, so what are the facts?' whispered Kip, trying to stay calm. 'The rangers aren't here and their line is dead. So, my guess is that the poachers found out about the trap and dealt with the rangers first. Which means that my dad is next on their list.' Kip looked at Ben. 'And what's the best way to get to my dad?'

'You!' whispered Ben.

'So, let's *give* them me.'

'You can't do that! Kip, they'll shoot you.'

'Not if *you* get to them first.'

'What?'

'I've had an idea, but we need to get inside first to see if it'll work. And how are we going to do that?'

'There's a way in round the back!' said Ben suddenly. 'Trevor calls it—'

'The Emergency Route! Nice one, bro! Let's go!'

CHAPTER 30

It didn't take them long, fuelled by adrenaline as they were, to go back down the hill, round the perimeter of the camp to the rear, and through the concealed back gate.

Then they both ran as quickly and quietly as possible, up the path towards the accommodation tents, and paused by one of the side paths for a moment.

'This is my tent,' said Ben. 'Why have we stopped here?'

'I'll just be a second. Wait for me here!' True to his word, Kip returned seconds later, carrying the spear from Ben's veranda. 'I've got a feeling you might need this,' he said, putting it in Ben's hand.

How different it felt to him now! He closed his hand around it and could feel the beginnings of a new kind of strength entering his body. He looked at Kip. 'Let's go!' he said.

They ran up the path towards the main area of the lodge, crouched over to keep out of sight, glancing all about them as they went. When they arrived at the last twist in the path before becoming visible, they slunk into the undergrowth to the left-hand side.

Their position was a good one, with a clear and protected view of the dining room. Ben's eyes focused immediately on the red shoes sticking out from behind the bar and they shone back like two warning signals. He longed to shout out to her, but he knew that would be the worst thing he could do. 'Move your feet!' he whispered. 'If you're still alive, Mum, move them. Please.'

Kip put his hand on Ben's back to silence him and so he pushed the anger down – deep down into his gut – and from there he could feel it radiating into his muscles, making them quiver in readiness.

He scanned the rest of the area but couldn't see Senteu anywhere. He glanced at Kip – had he noticed his father was missing? Ben could just make out the figures of Trevor, Phil and Jez, Surum the barman and some other lodge staff, all lying motionless on the dining-room floor. Standing over them, with his rifle aimed casually in their direction, was the gunman Ben had seen a week ago in the back of the pickup. And another man, in a red-brown T-shirt, with his back to the boys, was looking through Jez's pockets.

Ben watched as he pulled out a wallet from Jez's trousers, removed the money and stuffed it into his own pocket. Then he threw the wallet over his shoulder and sent credit cards flying everywhere. There was the faint sound of singing whilst he did this, and Ben was just beginning to wonder what kind of man would sing whilst pickpocketing someone, when he straightened up and his face became visible. Ben inhaled sharply, then Kip elbowed him and mouthed, 'Shetani!' But Ben already knew.

Then all of a sudden, Ben saw something that made his thumping heart almost stop completely.

The red shoes moved. They definitely moved.

Shetani's singing became louder and he started gesticulating like he was some sort of opera singer. He stepped to one side slightly whilst opening his arms wide as if making a grand finish and revealed Senteu who was sitting in an armchair behind him.

Kip breathed out.

'Senteu, Senteu, Senteu!' said Shetani with a large sigh. 'What are we going to do with you?'

Ben's stomach lurched at the sound of Shetani's voice. It was more like an English country gentleman than a gang leader – and there was something distinctly chilling about that.

'Well, my lovelies,' he continued, 'before we get started, I'd just like to check which language you'd prefer me to use. Do *you* speak many languages, Mr Camera Man?' Shetani made a melodramatic show of putting his hand to his ear and angling it towards Jez. 'Hmmm? What's that, I can't quite hear you?'

The sound of mumbling seemed to be coming from Jez. *Thank God*, thought Ben, *he's alive.*

'Oh!' exclaimed Shetani. 'Only English? Goodness! Well, I'm sure you speak it *very* well. I know six languages.' He counted them on his fingers. 'There's Kikuyu, Kiswahili, Maa, French, Chinese – and, er, oh yes, of course! English!'

The tone of his voice was making Ben feel sick.

Shetani pulled a slender, gold-tipped cigarette from the thigh pocket of his dirty khaki trousers and placed it between his lips, wafting the lighter around flamboyantly as he spoke.

'English it is, then.' He paused to light his cigarette. 'Good! So, Senteu, my dear boy! Now that we have liberated the most recent videotape from the confines of its recorder,' Shetani gestured to some pieces of camera equipment lying smashed in pieces on the ground, 'perhaps you feel ready to tell us where the rest of the footage is.'

'No!' said Senteu, calmly.

'Really?'

Senteu nodded.

'Irichi!' Shetani called the gunman, who passed him a metal bar that was lying on the ground. 'You still sure?' He waved the branding iron at Senteu as if he was trying to tempt him with something forbidden.

Ben looked at Kip. There was panic in his eyes.

'Oh, well, have it your own way,' said Shetani and with one swift movement he raised the bar up in the air and brought it down sharply on Senteu's arm.

And this time it was Ben stopping Kip from being heard. He grabbed the hand nearest to him and squeezed it as hard as he could whilst Kip punched the ground repeatedly with the other one.

'All right,' said Shetani, 'let me ask you again. Where is the footage?'

Why did he have to talk in that way, like a nurse or a schoolteacher? It made Ben's skin crawl.

'I am not going to tell *you*,' groaned Senteu, clutching his arm.

Shetani swung the bar with more force than the first time, and brought it down again in the same place. Then he let go of the cattle brand like a rapper dropping the mic.

Kip was now grinding the bones of Ben's hand against one another. It was excruciating, but Ben let him carry on.

'Oh, dear!' continued Shetani. 'Well, I'm sure the lady will respond to some . . .' he pretended to search for the words, '. . . gentle persuasion!' He raised his shoulders up to his ears and grinned, like he was just about to jump out and surprise someone on their birthday, then he rubbed his hands together gleefully and skipped over towards Kate.

CHAPTER 31

'No,' breathed Ben, 'No, No, NO—' He ripped his hand from Kip's grasp and grabbed the spear again. He held it tightly and it seemed to answer with an energy all of its own.

'I say, Kate, my dear,' gushed Shetani, 'your shoes are such fun!' He put the cigarette between his teeth, grabbed Kate by the feet, and dragged her out from behind the bar and across into the middle of the space. Irichi, the gunman, kept watch over everyone else, covering each person systematically with his rifle.

'Do not tell him anything, Senteu!' shouted Kate, trying to roll over. But Shetani held on to her ankles and braced himself against her so she couldn't move.

Ben scrambled to his feet.

'Not yet!' breathed Kip, pulling him back down before anyone saw.

Shetani sat down on Kate's back and began stroking her messy hair. 'Come on, poppet! You don't *really* want me to rearrange your face, do you?' He looked at her like he expected an answer. 'Still, cheaper than a facelift, I suppose. All right, as you wish!' He grabbed a handful of her hair, then yanked her head upwards.

'Stop!' shouted Senteu. 'Tent four – under the veranda floorboards.'

'No!' sobbed Kate.

'Thank you!' said Shetani in a sing-song voice, abruptly letting go of Kate's hair. Then he walked back towards Irichi.

'*Iko chini ya namba nne! Enda!*' Shetani said gruffly. The gunman immediately set off down the path towards Ben and Kip's hiding place.

'Irichi!' shouted Shetani after him. 'Rifle!' The gunman trotted back dutifully and held out the weapon to Shetani, who took it from him with a look of disgust, like he was being handed a dirty nappy.

When the gunman reached the point where the boys were hiding, the sound of blood rushing in Ben's ears was almost deafening, but the poacher walked briskly past, unaware of the tension in the grass to his right. The boys raised their heads again, slowly.

'Did you honestly think you could pull a trick like that on *me*?' Shetani hissed at Senteu. He seemed to have become a completely different person all of a sudden, but it wasn't just his voice that had changed. It was as if holding the rifle had pressed some kind of button, and all the performance had gone out of him. 'Do you think I am completely stupid or something?' He had bent right over and was spitting his words into Senteu's face. 'And the rangers? You thought they were impenetrable, I suppose? Idiot! Anyone can be bought with enough fear or money.'

The sound of heavy military boots on the path just behind the boys sent a fresh wave of terror through Ben's body, and he buried his head in the dirt again. But Irichi just jogged past them, still oblivious to their hiding place, with a camera bag dangling from his hand. When he reached the main area, he swapped the camera bag for the rifle, and took up his position again, pointing the gun at Senteu.

'Do you think I don't know where that brat Kipat is either?' Shetani continued. 'Back from his little jaunt with his grandfather, of course! Getting all cosy at the *manyatta*.'

Kip looked at Ben. There was a very small smile beginning to register on his face. 'Get ready, bro!' he whispered.

'You lied to me, Senteu,' Shetani breathed. 'You should not have done that. Because after I have dealt with you, I am going straight to the *manyatta* to finish the boy.' Then he threw his cigarette stub in Senteu's face and turned to leave, pausing only to give an order over his shoulder to Irichi.

'Shoot him!' he said.

'NO!' roared Kip. He bounded to his feet and sprinted down the path with Ben fast behind him. Within seconds the two boys were out in the open, and everyone turned to look.

Kip forked off to the left, leaving Ben with a clear view of the gunman.

Shetani whipped round at the sound of Kip's voice, only to see him leap into the air and clear the handful of steps that separated them. 'SHOOT HIM!' Shetani screamed.

Ben lowered his right arm down by his side and tightened his grip on the spear. He aimed his left arm at the rifle as Irichi swung it in Kip's direction. There was a deafening cracking sound, followed by the whistling of bullets, as Ben released the spear. Then, just before it made contact with its target, Irichi turned and pointed the rifle at Ben.

There was more rapid cracking and whistling, followed by the clanging of metal as the spear and the rifle collided. Then someone punched Ben in the shoulder. The force of it spun him round, lifted him off the ground and dropped him on his backside. He could barely breathe, but he just managed to turn back and see that the gunman was clutching his hand in agony and the rifle had fallen to the ground.

Senteu wasted no time. He grabbed the cattle brand from where Shetani had foolishly dropped it at his feet and swung it across Irichi's shins. Then, working in tandem, Trevor jumped on Irichi, grabbed his arm and twisted it behind his back in a half nelson. 'Got him!' he bellowed at Senteu. 'Go!'

Senteu grabbed the rifle and ran out after Shetani, who had made a bolt for the pickup.

And now Ben could no longer ignore the deep burning sensation in his shoulder, like someone had stabbed him with a red-hot skewer.

He looked down to where it was coming from, and groaned at the sight of blood oozing in a rhythmic pulse from a neat hole under his clavicle. The agony of it seemed to be increasing, but his throat had become so dry that he knew a scream would come to nothing.

'Ben!' said a familiar voice suddenly. 'Oh my God, Ben, you've been shot.'

'Mum!' he croaked. And an enormous sense of relief flooded through his body, emerging as a dry sob.

'It's OK,' she said, trying to get a look at the wound on his shoulder. 'It's OK, my darling, you're going to be OK.'

'Blimey, Twiglet!' said Jez, kneeling down at Ben's side, next to Kate and Phil, and catching sight of the blood.

'Where's Kip?' asked Ben.

Jez looked over his shoulder. 'Oh, no!' He stared, horror-stricken, at something off to the side. Ben tried to turn his head, not expecting for a moment that it would be Kip, lying there motionless on the ground.

CHAPTER 32

♦♦♦♦♦♦♦♦♦♦♦♦♦♦♦♦

They all ran to where Kip lay and Ben tried to follow, shuffling on his backside.

'No!' said Kate. But he ignored her and rolled over on to his knees. Painstakingly, he unfolded one leg after the other, wobbled to his feet and staggered the short distance to where his cousin lay strewn across the steps.

Kip's eyes were open, but they looked panicked, like he was struggling to breathe. There was bright red blood frothing from a wound in his chest. Then Ben heard it – a sucking sound coming from the wound. He knew what this was.

Unable to stand any longer, Ben fell back to his

knees at Kip's side and tried to use his hand to cover the wound, but he couldn't even feel his right arm, never mind lift it.

'Guys!' Ben urged. 'Help me sit him up.'

'Twiglet, you've been shot. You shouldn't move.'

'I have to!' he shouted. 'I *know* how to help him.'

Jez and Phil dragged Kip up to a sitting position at the bottom of the steps, and Ben moved in behind him, gritting his teeth against his own pain. Then, wishing he had his school ID badge with him, he clamped his left hand as tightly as he could on to the wound in Kip's chest. He could feel a sucking sensation against his hand, but frustratingly, it wasn't tight enough. Kip coughed weakly, and some blood spattered from his mouth on to his chin.

Trevor arrived and inhaled sharply. '*Ai!* It looks like we're going to need some serious help here. I'll call the Flying Doctors.'

There was a disconcerting rasping noise coming from Kip's throat now. He coughed again. More blood. Ben pulled his hand in harder, but it just wasn't creating a tight enough seal.

Blood was pouring out between his fingers and he could feel the tunnels closing in around his eyes as his blood pressure began to drop.

'No!' screamed Ben as loudly as he could, desperately trying to summon up his anger. The feeling was coming back in his right arm now, and although it hurt like hell, at least he could move it.

'I need a card,' he shouted. And no sooner were the words out of his mouth than he noticed Jez's credit cards scattered on the ground.

'Yes! Jez, give me one of those cards! Quick!' Ben clamped the card to the wound. The effect was immediate: Kip gasped, taking in great lungfuls of air, but then seconds later his head flopped down on to his chest like a rag doll.

'Phil!' Ben yelled again. 'Your belt!'

Phil stripped off his belt in one move; it cracked loudly like the lash of a whip. Then he helped Ben tie the card on to the wound as tightly as he could, hands shaking, whilst Kate held Kip's head up. And to Ben's utmost relief, his cousin began to breathe again.

'Right!' said Trevor. 'I've just spoken to the Flying Doctors and the Medevac plane is here in the Mara already. If we can just get you to the airstrip they can fly us out. The only problem is, we have to get there before dark, and it's an hour's drive away.'

'Can you get there faster?' asked Kate.

'*I* can!' said Senteu, suddenly appearing in front of them.

'Senteu!' exclaimed Kate. 'Where's Shetani?'

'I tied him to a post in reception. The driver escaped with the pickup, but I got this,' he said, holding the camera bag aloft.

'Oh! Thank you!' Kate sighed.

Then Senteu caught sight of Kip and he dropped to his knees in front of him, his face stricken with horror. 'Kipat!' he said, 'My boy, can you hear me?' There was no response.

'We need to go NOW if we're going to get these boys on the plane,' said Trevor.

'I'll get the Land Cruiser,' cried Senteu, and he bounded off.

As if in response to his father leaving him, Kip's breathing became shallower and shallower, until eventually it was barely perceptible.

'Stay awake, Kip!' Ben shouted, pinching and shaking him. 'Please stay awake!'

As he shook him again, Kip's toga slipped to one side, revealing another wound on his leg. Ben gasped. There was no neat entry wound here, just a mess of flesh, blood and even bone. How could a little bullet do so much damage? Ben retched and his head began to spin again.

'NO!' he shouted again. 'This is NOT HAPPEN-ING NOW!'

And from somewhere deep inside him he felt a gathering force of anger at last. It began as a low growl that built into a huge roar, catapulting him into a burst of superhuman strength. In one fluid movement, Ben rose to his feet, pulling his cousin up on to his good shoulder in a fireman's lift.

'What are you doing?' shouted his mum, but Ben was entirely focused on the task in front of him. He stamped up each step, digging in his toes as went, then pressed on determinedly to the front of the lodge. And just as he arrived, in a moment of perfect timing, Senteu pulled up in the Land Cruiser.

Trevor lunged forward and opened the passenger door. Ben lowered Kip inside as carefully as he could, then squeezed in behind him, so he could keep the credit card tightly clamped on the wound.

'You must get there before dusk,' said Trevor, closing the door. 'The plane won't be able to take off after that.'

As they drove off, Ben caught sight of Shetani. He

was tied to the base of an entrance pillar – hands behind him, head turned away. Then, as if he sensed he was being watched, he moved his eyes – but only his eyes – and locked them on to Ben's like a sniper. And for the few seconds that they stared at each other, it felt like Shetani was slowly pushing his finger into the bullet wound in Ben's shoulder.

'Don't bother about him,' said Ben's mum, from the back seat. 'You'll never have to clap eyes on that piece of evil again.'

Senteu drove faster and faster, and Ben pushed his chest out to keep Kip's back straight and the card tight on the wound, but the pain in his shoulder was becoming impossible to ignore. When the car hit a bump at a bad angle, Kip's head banged against Ben's wound, making him cry out in pain. Kip's mouth fell open and a trickle of blood ran down his chin. Then his breath became raspy and shallow again, like it might be reaching its end. Ben pulled the credit card tighter.

As they drove, he looked down at the horror movie that was his cousin's leg. There was a white flag of bone protruding from the wound and, though the blood was not actually pumping out, both their togas were soaked in it.

He tried to find a pulse on Kip's wrist. Nothing. His neck. Nothing. And as he sat there, trying desperately to think of something else to do to save his cousin's life, he suddenly felt absolutely overwhelmed with tiredness, as though someone had just covered him with a lead blanket. And he was cold. So cold.

The Land Cruiser came to a stop and some people opened his door. Somewhere very far away, was the sound of an aircraft engine.

'No,' he tried to say, 'we have to keep going – we must get to the plane – I think he's dying.'

But the people weren't listening. They were pulling Kip away. Ben tried to hold on, but he was just too weak, too tired to fight. And as the darkness began to close around him, he had no choice but to let go.

CHAPTER 33

Ben woke suddenly.

There was something banging on the inside of his brain with a heavy, dull thud, and his right shoulder felt as though it had been run over by a tank.

He had a hazy memory of watching blood oozing between the digits of his left hand. He tried to lift his head to get a closer look, but it was like trying to support a bowling ball on a liquorice stick. Determined to see the evidence, he raised his hand to his face instead. It felt weak, but was completely clean. The only trace of blood was on the plaster that held the drip needle in place.

And as Ben began to understand his whereabouts,

everything else came flooding back too, as though a very loud and alarmingly bright video was beginning to stream in his mind's eye. How could he have let himself fall asleep? He could see Kip's face, panicked from the lack of air. He could hear his last few breaths before he stopped breathing altogether. He could feel his cousin's lifeblood, warm and sticky in his hands as Ben tried desperately to find the pulse that wasn't there.

If only he'd been quicker with the spear, Kip would still be alive. If he hadn't been such a useless wimp about the whole blood thing and passed out, then he would have got Kip to the aeroplane on time. Not only had he failed to beat his fear of blood, but his cousin was dead because of it.

Kip's grinning face filled Ben's head, and the dam wall that was holding back all his feelings began to crack, allowing hot tears to roll silently down his face. He'd only known Kip for a week, but he was the best friend he'd ever had. Now he was gone, and it was all Ben's fault.

The door squeaked open and his mum walked in, bathed in a halo of light from outside. Ben looked away.

'So,' she said in a bright voice, 'my Maasai warrior

is awake.'

'Don't, Mum!'

'Come on Ben, I'm proud of you.'

'Why? I'm not a warrior. I don't deserve to be alive.'

'Ben, that's not—'

'I'm useless. I'm just a useless waste of —'

'Can you stop whining, please?' said a voice at Ben's side. 'You're giving me a headache.'

Ben immediately forgot the pain in his shoulder and turned to where the voice was coming from. And there, lying in the bed next to him, was his cousin, the usual silly grin on his face.

'Kip!' cried Ben. 'I thought you were dead.'

'Dead? No way, I've had the best medical help known to Maasai.'

'The Flying Doctors, you mean? Did you get on the plane? I thought we didn't make it.'

'No, you idiot, I'm talking about you.'

'What?'

'He's right, Ben,' said his mum. 'The Flying Doctors got you both to Nairobi hospital, but it was you that saved Kip's life. The doctor in charge said that if you hadn't done the thing with the credit card, Kip would have died within minutes.'

The door opened again and a woman in a white coat walked briskly up to Ben's bed.

'Ben,' said his mum, 'this is Dr Kiburio, who flew with you to Nairobi on the AMREF plane.'

'Hello,' the woman said. Her voice was clear and reassuringly confident. 'Glad to see the Flying Doctor is awake and well!'

'Hello,' said Ben, his face flushing slightly.

'Now, where did you learn how to respond to a sucking chest wound?'

'At school, in our first aid class.'

'Well good for you for remembering what to do. Most people forget their first aid training immediately.'

'Really?' asked Kate.

'Absolutely!' replied the doctor. 'You clearly have a natural aptitude for medicine, Benedict, and the kind of unflappable nature that is perfect for a Flying Doctor. Have you ever thought about the medical profession?'

'Ha!' said Ben's mum. 'Funny you should say that!'

'Yeah, Doc,' interjected Kip, 'it's his dream to be a doctor.'

'Then how about becoming a Flying Doctor?' Dr Kiburio asked.

'I can't!' croaked Ben, and the doctor raised her eyebrows. 'I have a blood phobia. I can't be a doctor, never mind a flying one. I didn't even make it to the plane without passing out.'

'If I may interrupt you, my Maasai friend,' said Dr Kiburio, 'there is no way that someone who is not in control of a blood phobia could have saved your cousin's life the way you did.'

'See!' said Ben's mum.

'The only reason you passed out,' the doctor continued, 'was because you had lost so much blood yourself. You went into shock. It's the body's natural way of preserving itself, but then you'll learn about that in medical school.'

'Yes, bro!' exclaimed Kip.

'Another thing you will discover, is that a fear of blood will not stop you from becoming a doctor. There will be others with the phobia on your course – there certainly were when I was training – and they are all excellent doctors now – some are even surgeons.'

'Are you listening to this, cuz?' asked Kip. Ben wished he could throw something at him.

'It is most unusual for someone of your age to have learnt how to handle their fear of blood already, never mind rescue someone with a life-threatening blood injury. It all bodes well for you becoming a very fine doctor indeed. You must promise me one thing, however.'

'What's that?' Ben whispered, now in a different kind of shock altogether.

'That, once you have trained, you will come back and work for the Flying Doctors.'

Ben looked at his mum and cousin, they both nodded encouragingly.

'OK,' he replied, weakly.

'Good!' said Dr Kiburio, satisfied at last. 'Now, I will go because there are a lot of people waiting outside and you will need to take a rest soon.' Then she smiled at everyone and left as briskly as she had arrived.

'Did that just happen?' asked Ben.

'You'd better believe it,' said Kip.

'Are there really people here? To see *me*?'

'Of course!' said Ben's mum.

'Is Uncle Senteu here? And Grandpapi?'

'Yes. They're waiting outside with everyone else.'

'Who's everyone else?'

'Granny Koko, Jez, Phil, Trevor, everyone! I'll call them in, shall I?'

'No, Mum, wait a minute,' said Ben. 'What happened with the rangers? Why didn't they turn up?'

She sighed. 'It's so sad. Shetani had turned one of them – probably threatened his family like he did with Senteu. When the rangers were about to set off for the lodge, Shetani's ally followed his new boss's orders and locked them all in a prison cell at the base then ran away.'

'And the poachers?'

'We got all of them – except the driver, of course, but he'll turn up.'

'So where's Shetani now?'

'In Nairobi prison, awaiting trial.'

Ben shivered as if someone had walked over his grave.

His mum put her hand on his arm. 'You were brave, my love,' she said. 'Both of you boys – very brave.' She smiled at them. 'So, can I call everyone in now? Are you strong enough?'

Ben didn't care whether he was strong enough; he felt like he was in some sort of dream. He nodded, and she opened the door and beckoned them inside.

Koipapi was the first to enter, followed by Senteu, then Granny Koko, Jez, Trevor and three elders that Ben recognized from the homecoming ceremony. One of them was carrying a spear.

The grey room was filled with a vibrant burst of colour, as though someone had turned on the light and the now familiar yet comforting smell of cow hit Ben's senses, overpowering the clinical odour of hospital disinfectant.

His eyes immediately locked with Senteu's.

'Benedict,' his uncle said gently, 'I have wronged you. Before you were even born, I robbed you of the joy of knowing your father.' He lowered himself to his knees. 'Benedict, my brother's son, my own blood, can you ever find it in your heart to forgive me?'

The room was absolutely silent, save for the intermittent beeping of the heart monitors.

'Yes!' whispered Ben. 'Of course.'

Senteu gazed up at him and Ben realized that he had been wrong about his uncle all along. What he thought had been anger when they first met, he now knew to be sorrow. Deep sorrow. And he was sure about this because, for the first time in his own life, Ben knew what it might be like to lose a brother and a best friend. But he could see the sadness beginning to leave his uncle's eyes, and a smile growing in its place – for the first time in thirteen years.

'Thank you!' Senteu said, rising to his feet. 'And I also want to thank you, Benedict, for giving us your cows.'

Ben looked quizzically at Kip.

'I told him, bro.'

'You are brave like your father,' Senteu continued, 'but you have also inherited the blessing of your mother's kindness. Kipat and I will love your herd like our own until you return for them.'

Then Ben's grandfather stepped forward and laid his hand on Ben's head.

'*Ormuranikiti!*' he said, then again two more times, whilst keeping his hand in place. '*Ormuranikiti! Ormuranikiti!*'

Ben glanced at his mum – there were tears streaming down her face – then at Kip, whose eyes were filling up too. *What was wrong with everyone?*

'Your grandfather has given you a Maasai name,' said Senteu.

'What does it mean?' asked Ben, hoping it wasn't a rude question.

'Warrior Boy,' Senteu said.

Ben looked back at his mum, who was now smiling *and* crying!

Grandpapi stepped forward again, but this time he had in his hand the spear that the elder had been carrying.

'And now,' said Senteu, 'to you who saved my son's life, to you, bravest of all warriors, Benedict Olmoran, we give you your father's spear.'

Koipapi jabbed the spear up into the air above Ben's head three times, and Granny Koko ululated with all her might. Then, as his grandmother's stirring victory holler died down, Koipapi leant the spear against Ben's bedside table, obviously understanding that he couldn't take it with his right hand just now.

'Bro,' said Kip, 'I've got something to give you too.' He reached gingerly under his hospital gown and pulled out the small, smooth stone he'd used when his blood phobia was bad.

'But that's your special stone, I can't take that,' said Ben.

'Yeah you can, it'll remind you of where you come from. And you never know, maybe you'll meet a girl one day, who you might like to think about when you ...' he rubbed the stone suggestively, then threw it neatly on to Ben's bed.

'You are so weird,' said Ben, embarrassed that his

mum and grandparents were listening. 'But seriously though, where do you keep all that stuff – your phone and that?'

'Maasai secret!' said Kip. 'You'll have to come back to Kenya for more training. I will reveal all then.'

'I don't think I'll ever be ready for that!'

'Right, then,' said a nurse, coming into the room. 'That's enough excitement for one day, these boys need their rest.'

Ben had only been awake for twenty minutes but he already felt like he could sleep for a week, and Kipat was beginning to slur his words like a drunk.

One by one, every person in the room came over and touched the boys on the head, speaking their blessing before leaving.

'I knew you'd do it, bro,' said Kip, drowsily, once everyone had left. 'Do you want to know why I had such confidence?' Ben nodded, even though Kip couldn't really see because his eyes were closing. 'There is an old Maasai saying that tells how Ngai would never be so cruel as to make someone ugly *and* a coward.'

Ben opened his mouth to protest, but Kip was already snoring.

CHAPTER 34

As the jumbo jet climbed steadily upwards into the cloudless blue sky, Ben thought about how different things were now.

It was nearly three weeks since he'd sat in his kitchen in London, wondering about Kenya. He'd have given anything then to have been able to read the future. But if he'd known what lay ahead, he wouldn't have come. And if he hadn't come, he never would have met them. His family.

It wasn't just his fear of blood that they had helped him with – they'd given him something else too. Kip's question about whether he felt more black or white, more one thing or another, had been quietly whispering to him since his cousin had asked it. And now Ben was beginning to think an answer might be revealing itself.

The slim chance that he'd ever had of fitting in at school would be a lot narrower now. No one in his class had a blood phobia, but neither did they have cow-herding skills or a Maasai warrior's spear. He was more 'different' now than ever, but it didn't seem to matter to him like it had before, because now he was a part of something.

His mum sat next to him, discussing the elephant project with Jez as usual. Her freckled, creamy-coloured hands were dancing to the rhythm of her argument, expressing her point passionately. Her wild blonde hair, still untameable.

Ben wiggled the fingers of his right hand sticking out of his sling – so much darker now that he'd spent all that time in the sun. He wondered who the other passengers thought he was. Her adopted son, perhaps, visiting his African birthplace for the first time? But they couldn't possibly know what he and his mum really shared just by looking. It was hidden treasure.

He had more memories from the last few weeks than he could count, but the one that stuck with him more than any other was the baby elephant clinging to its dead mother in the clearing. He could see it when he closed his eyes, and though he would have liked to be able to erase the horror of it from his mind, he was pleased that he now understood what his mum felt so strongly about.

'What do you think, sweetheart?' she said, suddenly.

'About what?'

'Well, the guys and I are discussing, our story. I don't feel we've got it right yet.'

'Ah, come on,' argued Jez. 'We have the bones of a good film, I think.'

'Exactly!' said Phil. 'Only the bones. I agree with Kate – I'm concerned that it's not going to change anything.'

'Why don't you show your films to the people who buy the ivory?' said Ben. And everyone looked at him like he had just spoken for the first time in his life. 'Kip says most Chinese people don't know that elephants are killed for their tusks.'

'Go on,' urged his mum.

'Well if you show them what really happens, then maybe they won't want to buy it any more.'

'So just change the audience, or the story as well?' asked his mum.

'You could focus on the baby elephants, struggling to survive without their mothers. You'd have to be pretty mean to buy ivory if you knew about that.'

'That's a good angle, Twiglet,' said Jez.

'It's Warrior Boy to you,' Kate said, patting Ben proudly on the knee.

The plane banked slightly to the left, and Ben could feel the stone his cousin had given him pressing into his leg. He reached into his pocket and held it between his fingers, watching through the tiny window as the ground drew further away. The stone belonged down there and its job, Kip had said, was to remind Ben that he did too. At least part of him.

He had already decided on the perfect place to keep it – next to the photo of his dad on the chest of drawers in his bedroom. He couldn't wait to get home and look at the picture again, through new eyes.

Home.

He was actually looking forward to going home.

So perhaps that was the answer to the question – he was both. Both Maasai and English, both black and white. Yes, that felt right. He still wasn't sure where he fitted in at school, especially having missed two extra weeks of it, but at least he fitted in with himself.

'Ben!' said his mum. 'How do you feel about coming back to Kenya and helping us make the next film?'

Ben looked at Jez and Phil who were smiling and nodding in agreement.

'Let me think about it,' he said, and turned his gaze back to the red earth now far below him, secure in the knowledge that one day, he would walk upon it again.

The warm evening sun lay low in the sky, streaking the horizon with the hues of possibility. A gentle breeze stirred the sea of grass on the savannah below him, then, a moment later, stroked his skin.

Just a few strides away, the lion stood, gazing majestically at the same landscape, his mane lifted by the same wind. He raised his chin slightly as if sensing the future.

Then, without making a sound, they both turned and walked towards the setting sun.

ABOUT THE BOOK

A few years ago, I was teaching in a school in Nairobi, when a new student from England joined my class. His family were Kenyan but he had never visited the country before. Being from London, he was considered cool, but also extremely different. I wondered how it would feel to be him. Did he enjoy being different? Did his family as well as his friends find him strange? What would happen to him if he couldn't fit in? And this is when Ben's story began to emerge.

So, I set out to write a book about a boy – I certainly wasn't thinking about elephants when I began – but they have a habit of barging in, uninvited. I comfort myself, though, with the thought that a love of elephants came as a surprise to Ben too.

There are many great elephant conservation organizations operating in Africa but being on this journey with Ben has led me to the wonderful Mara Elephant Project (MEP), who work tirelessly to protect elephants from the constant threat of poaching in the Maasai Mara.

Sometimes, wildlife charities can be so focused on saving animals, that they forget about humans.

MEP are funded by the Escape Foundation who have a reassuring interest in both. If you would like to know more about MEP or Escape, please take a look at www.maraelephantproject.org and www.escape foundation.org respectively.

To read further about the Maasai tribe, you can try Tepilit Saitoti's book *Maasai* which is totally brilliant and has great pictures, but it weighs a tonne, so whilst you wait for your warrior muscles to develop, you could check out the Maasai Association website at www.maasai-association.org

I hope you enjoyed *Warrior Boy* and that it has inspired you to dig a little deeper into your own heritage or take up the javelin . . . or both!

ACKNOWLEDGEMENTS

Tepilit Saitoti who wrote *Maasai* – for teaching me about the Maasai love of cows, God, children and laughter. What more is there? Nigel Pavitt, for introducing me to Tepilit's work in the beginning. Jackson Looseyia, Newton Koipapi, Mzee Karianini and Martin Kasaine for helping me understand what it is to be a warrior. Jared Opiyo for the emergency translation text messages and Talash Saroni for the beautiful Maasai saying.

Bertie Haywood, Luke Evans and Oscar Cheffings – for giving me a much-valued teenager's perspective on our *manyatta* trip. Dom Troulan for teaching me about gunshot wounds but, more importantly, how to perform the Vulcan neck grip.

Mike Pflanz, Gemma Francis and Richard Roberts – for answering my myriad questions. To Brian Kearney-Grieve and Claire Bolles at Escape – for your wonderful warmth in adopting *Warrior Boy* without hesitation. Tilda Bowden – for the blood phobia and hair colour advice.

Rob Bell for teaching me to listen, Elizabeth Gilbert for teaching me to listen out for stories and

Uncle Senteu, for teaching me to listen to character.

Zoe King for 'seeing' this story and my agent Josephine Hayes for seeing it through.

A heartfelt thank you goes to everyone at Chicken House – Victoria Walters for your astoundingly keen eye and kindness in delivering suggestions. Barry Cunningham, Elinor Bagenal, Rachel Hickman, Esther Waller, Rachel Leyshon, Kesia Lupo, Jazz Bartlett and Laura Myers for your consummate wisdom, patience and grace.

Jess and Bridge – for laughs, tea, tears and rusks.

To Mum and Dad for teaching me perseverance.

And finally to Justin, Amelia and PJ. For all those times I said no to film night. Prepare for a back-to-back *Stars Wars* bonanza!

BELOW ZERO by DAN SMITH

When Zak's plane crash-lands on Outpost Zero, a small Antarctic research base in one of the most isolated places on Earth, he discovers a cold, dark nightmare. The power's out and the people who live there have disappeared. Worse, as he searches for answers, bizarre visions suggest a link to something else – deep beneath the ice – which only he can understand . . .

Paperback, ISBN 978-1-910655-92-4, £6.99 • ebook, ISBN 978-1-911077-55-8, £6.99